CROCODILE BURNING

Mosake, the director, speaks to us.

"This is a plastic crocodile, but to all of you here, for a moment at least, it was frighteningly real. It was a monster with the power to startle and confuse you. And why? Because it's the shape of one of our African myths, iSezela—the old, evil crocodile that lies in the shallow water ready to attack the innocent.

"Our country is filled with plastic crocodiles: the old traditions that enslave our people, the educational system, the government and its policies, detention without trial, the State of Emergency, and the crime and violence in our townships. This is what our musical is about. And you—you are the young people who have the power to change everything."

His words have punched a hole through my head and awakened me. No one has ever spoken so powerfully to me before.

CROCODILE BURNING

MICHAEL WILLIAMS

PUFFIN BOOKS

*I want to thank Rosemary Brosnan
for her editorial care,
Eithne Doherty for her initial guidance,
Amy Kaplan for her enduring friendship,
Lungille Jacobs for his eye for detail,
and Vanessa O'Connor for her loving patience.*

No character in this book is intended to represent any actual person;
all the incidents of the story are entirely fictional in nature.

PUFFIN BOOKS
Published by the Penguin Group
Penguin Books USA Inc., 375 Hudson Street, New York, New York 10014, U.S.A.
Penguin Books Ltd, 27 Wrights Lane, London W8 5TZ, England
Penguin Books Australia Ltd, Ringwood, Victoria, Australia
Penguin Books Canada Ltd, 10 Alcorn Avenue, Toronto, Ontario, Canada M4V 3B2
Penguin Books (N.Z.) Ltd, 182-190 Wairau Road, Auckland 10, New Zealand

Penguin Books Ltd, Registered Offices: Harmondsworth, Middlesex, England

First published in the United States of America by Lodestar Books,
an affiliate of Dutton Children's Books, a division of Penguin Books USA Inc., 1992
Published in Puffin Books, 1994

1 3 5 7 9 10 8 6 4 2

THE LIBRARY OF CONGRESS HAS CATALOGED THE LODESTAR BOOKS EDITION AS FOLLOWS:

Williams, Michael
Crocodile burning / Michael Williams. p. cm.
Summary: South African teenager Seraki joins the cast of
a musical written to express rage at conditions in his township
and travels to perform it in New York.
ISBN 0-525-67401-2
[1. South Africa—Fiction. 2. Theater—Fiction.
3. Blacks—South Africa—Fiction.] I. Title.
PZ7.W66715Cr 1992 [Fic]—dc20 91-46197 CIP AC

Puffin Books ISBN 0-14-036793-4

Printed in the United States of America

OTHER PUFFIN BOOKS YOU MAY ENJOY

THE RED SPORTS CAR

Early this morning I saw a dead cat lying on the side of the road with all its fur taken off. I stopped to look at it, crouched down, and studied its skin. Its head was turned away from me, and already ants were pricking at its ears. Across the road a skinny, almost dead dog was watching me with jealous eyes, waiting for me to leave. I poked the cat with a stick, turned it over, and inspected its stomach. Not the ants, not the dog, not even I could do anything to it anymore. It was like a pink, naked baby, deader than dead, which had gone to a place beyond pricking, beyond poking, and beyond pain.

Later, when I arrived at the Ikwezi Railway Station, I saw a dead man lying in the road. He was naked too. Somebody had torn up a black plastic bin liner and put it over him, but his thick, calloused toes stuck out. A man in a floppy hat and baggy pants said he was killed in the night by the Naughty Boys and that they took all his clothes.

I pushed through the crowd and crouched down to get a closer look at him, but was shoved away by an adult who knew better.

An old woman said that children shouldn't see things like this. I had seen a skinned cat and worse, and anyway I was no longer a child.

"These *tsotsis* have no souls," the old woman said to her friend, as they walked away from the circle of people around the dead man.

"They could have at least left him his underwear," the friend replied.

"And his shoes."

"Ai, we are nothing to them."

"You're right, *sisi*. We are nothing to these *tsotsis*."

1

At least they left him his skin. If they'd taken that too, he'd be pink like the dead cat, but instead he looked like a sleeping black man. He looked a little like Phakane, my brother.

I missed the train to school because I watched a taxi take the dead man away to the mortuary and because I was thinking about Phakane. I've seen dead men before, but never a cat with its fur taken off. Nobody cares about a skinned cat lying in the road, and I didn't feel like going to school anymore so I went home and had a fight with my mother.

I told her about the dead man that looked like Phakane and the skinned cat, and why I missed the train. It all made sense to me, but she started crying, and then she shouted at me. She said she was going to call the teachers to come and fetch me. I said, If you call them I still won't go, because they talk nonsense.

I wanted her to leave me alone. I don't need school with its useless teachers, its crammed classrooms, its special Black Education, and its stupid boycotts.

Seraki, you are just like your father, she said. And then I got really mad. No one must ever say I am like Mr. Nzule. I shouted at her that Mr. Nzule is someone else. I am me. Not like anyone, and certainly not like Mr. Nzule.

My mother kept quiet and went off to work for her rich madam. She is too tired to fight properly with me nowadays.

So I went to see a girlfriend. I knew she would be at home because she feels the same way about school as I do. When I tried to kiss her she had many excuses that made no sense. I left her because she can be stupid sometimes.

Now I am sitting alone at our kitchen window, thinking about my brother and looking out at our yard. It is bare ground, trodden hard and swept clean to keep the dust away. There has been no rain this winter, and the ground is cracked, and the air dry. It's not really our yard, or our kitchen window, or even a proper house. We live in a three-room tin shanty behind Mrs. Mcebi's house because she does not ask too much money for rent, and because Mr. Nzule is lazy.

One day I will sit in a kitchen of my own house. It will be a big house with walls made of brick and cement, and painted white on both the outside and the inside. The house will have electricity and water, and the roof will not be held on by old engine blocks and bricks like this one is. Instead, it will be a solid, even roof with a tall, silver TV antenna. I will definitely own a television one day.

From that kitchen window I will see the neat rows of my vegetable garden, and when I walk out of that kitchen, I will pass through many large rooms. Each will have its own purpose, and every person in my house will have their own room. It will take a whole minute of walking before I get to my room, and when I get there I will go through a doorway instead of only past a curtain. All the rooms in my house will have doors, real doors, solid doors that can be closed.

Outside my bedroom window will be another garden with a lawn and fruit trees and flowers. Beyond all that green, on the driveway, will be my car. It will be red—not a dull red like our tin roof, but flash-red like fire engines, a red that says: I'm here, I'm bright and bold and fast, and I'm going places.

I can see every detail of the silver hubcaps and the red finish on the body of the car, with shiny silver strips on the sides that will make it look like it is going fast even when it is only sitting still waiting for me.

I will walk proudly to my car, open the door, and drop into the bucket seat. It will be made of leather, and the leather will smell so new that I'll have to control myself and take only small sniffs so as not to use up the newness too quickly.

The black driving gloves will be made from leather, too, and they'll wait on the dashboard behind the steering wheel. My knuckles will come through the holes cut for them, and when I have the gloves on, they will fit the shape of my hands perfectly.

Then I'll slide my key into the ignition and turn on the engine of my shiny red sports car. When it begins to purr, it will tell me of the places we will go—Cape Town, Harare, Nairobi—anywhere, everywhere there is a road to take us.

Roads and places in dreams are like that: so real that when you wake up and they're not there, they make you want to cry.

I know how stupid it is to daydream like this, but I often do it. Maybe it's a bad habit, but when I think of my brother, I want to stop thinking altogether, and so I make up good thoughts to drive away the bad ones. Good thoughts like the one I made up just now, about the house I will live in someday and the shiny red sports car parked in my driveway.

It's very hot in this kitchen, and the roof and walls tick as the sun twists the corrugated iron. The room smells of sour milk, dust, and Mr. Nzule's *muti*-medicine. Sitting here, I've already killed five flies with my bare hands. They're lying in a neat pile in front of me on the table. My next victim is walking on the window frame, trying to get outside, to escape down the narrow alley past Mrs. Mcebi's house and fly over the other houses and shanties of Soweto.

Mr. Nzule will come down that alley shortly, and I should be thinking about what I'm going to say to him. He'll be surprised to find me at home on Friday. As he walks in he will growl at me and say, Seraki, what are you doing here? Why aren't you at school? And I'll answer, We were told to boycott classes today. It's the August boycott. We have to have at least one every week and we're starting early this month.

He won't believe me, of course. He doesn't believe anything I tell him—not since the trouble with the stolen cars.

There is no point in my telling Mr. Nzule anything. He won't believe that they don't teach us much that matters in school, that we never have complete lessons because of teacher or student boycotts, that there are not enough desks, not enough books, not enough paper, not enough of anything.

He will look at me, twist his mouth, snort, and come out with one of his usual stupid sayings like, He's the fool who thinks he knows everything and makes excuses because he knows nothing. And while he's speaking I'll stare back at him in just the way that makes him most angry, and then get out of his way before he can find a stick or throw something at me.

Now I can hear his voice coming up the alley. There's a woman

4

with him. I don't know this one. She's young and pretty, and walks on high heels. She's laughing up at him, and he's smiling back at her. I know that smile. He's just said something he thinks is clever and is pleased with himself.

I hear him apologizing to her about our house. He's telling her he's going to rent one of the new government houses and that he's only living here until he gets something he really likes. It's always the same old story.

The smell of the sour milk is strong in the kitchen. I put the tip of my thumb over the wriggling fly and slowly press down. This is another reason I'm often angry with my mother. She knows about Mr. Nzule's women, but she does nothing about it. She allows him to bring women here when she's at work, and then pretends not to notice their smell they leave behind.

If I move now, I can be out the back window without their knowing I've seen them. They're almost at the door. If I stay, his smile will turn into a frown when he opens the door, and then to a scowl, as I stare him and his woman down.

I shove my chair back noisily, on purpose, kick over the table, and leap out through the back window. I dash across the yard and run down the alley out into the street. It is crowded with people just off the 3:15 train from the city. They move down the road like peas rolling out of a can. The minibuses are lined up like horses ready to race, and the drivers shout their destinations as the crowd moves toward them. People shout back, haggle with the drivers, and are stuffed with their shopping parcels, ten, twelve, maybe even fourteen, into the minibuses, which speed away to all the zones in the township.

I feel great knowing Mr. Nzule won't like what happened just now. He'll say bad things about my mother to this woman, and then he'll clean up the house because he feels guilty. He has a hard time explaining his other women to my mother, but he'll find a way of getting back at me. Mr. Nzule always does. This is not the first time I've caught him out. He's supposed to be looking for work, fixing our house, and selling toothpaste to Auntie Somoza's customers, but instead he's looking for women and quick cash. Phakane says the system has broken Mr. Nzule, but I know that's not true. Mr. Nzule is stupid and lazy. He's broken himself.

I stop running, and wait at the side of the road for a Pick 'n Pay truck, which is weaving its way slowly through the hurrying people. It is easy to scramble up to the foothold on its back bumper, and to hold on to the lock of its doors. I like being above the crowd, feeling the wind in my face, and moving fast as the truck picks up speed. The swirling dust of the open road pricks my eyes, but I shout over the roar of the truck's engine as the speed lifts me and carries me away from home. And then I think of Phakane and I want to let go and fall back to the ground. I want to be tossed and bruised and feel the cut of the stones and broken bottles that litter the roadway as I hit the earth. I wish I had money, lots of money. I wish I were far away, beyond everything: naked, skinned, and dead.

"Hey, you! Get off there!"

I turn my head to the side and blink the dust from my eyes. A shiny red sports car has come up behind my truck. A fat man is leaning his head out the window and shouting at me. The driver's blowing the hooter. The fat man shouts again.

"Get off there! You'll kill yourself!"

The car pulls alongside me. I stare at it, pretending not to understand what the man is shouting.

"Hey, did you hear? Get off!"

The car moves ahead. The driver shrugs and waves at me. His companion rolls up his window, shaking his head. The car's exactly the kind of red I like—like fire engines! I edge along the back of the truck, stretching around its corner to peer after my red sports car.

Then the truck wheel beneath me jolts into a deep rut, and my foot jumps free and drags on the rushing ground. I cling desperately to the lock and pull myself back up onto the truck and tighten my grip. Sweat burns my eyes and trickles down my neck. The truck's moving too fast now. I look for a way off, but cars are following too close behind, and beside the road there's only a blur of dusty, hard ground and gravel.

A van is trying to overtake us. Its driver keeps his hand on the hooter, and my truck slows down to let him pass. Now's my chance.

I jump, hit the ground, stumble, and fall free of the traffic. I lie gasping for air to fill my chest and slowly feel pain in many places. I've scraped and torn my arm, cut my leg, and my brains are swinging about inside my head. I stagger to my feet and force myself to focus on the image of a red sports car. I shake my head and rub the haze from my eyes. I can't believe what I see. There, in front of me, stands the shiny red sports car.

AUDITION

There it stands, just as I had imagined. It is the bold, fancy red I like, and it has the same fat wheels and silver hubcaps that I dreamed of. Except now it's parked outside a battered old building instead of in my driveway. I limp across the road to get a closer look.

Some little kids are gawking at their reflections in the gleaming hood. I push past them as I move slowly around my car. A pair of driving gloves is lying—just as I had imagined—on the leather bucket seat. Other boys are stroking the handles, smearing their snotty noses on the windows, and making sounds of an engine roaring. I want to push them away, tell them not to touch my car. Instead, I stand apart and watch them mess all over this red sports car that sped past me.

Behind me, people are going into the building. It looks like some kind of community center. I recognize a popular tune coming from the open door.

"What's going on in there?" I ask one of the boys.

"It's Mosake. He's got this hall for his musical."

"Who's Mosake?"

"I don't know, but he drives this car. Sharp, hey?"

"He's a director," says another boy. "He works in the city, in the white man's theater. He's even been on TV!"

"How much do you think it'd cost?" the first boy asks.

"A hundred thousand rand!"

These boys know nothing. A hundred thousand rand! Nothing in the world can cost that much money.

I walk toward the entrance of the building. I want to see the man who owns my car. From the back of the Pick 'n Pay truck I only saw the fat man with the open mouth.

Smartly dressed people walk into the building as if they're going into a church. One of the girls pushes past me and stares. Why's she looking at me like that?

Because I'm dusty and bleeding and everyone else is so clean.

Most of the girls are wearing new dresses: their hair is tinted with highlights, their shoes are shiny and black. And the boys, too, leaning up against the outside wall watching the girls, are dressed up and ready for a party, like in the commercials on TV. Next to them, I look like a dirty rag and I don't belong here, but I only want to see the man who owns my car before I go.

I move to just inside the doorway. Everyone's talking and laughing, and several people are standing around a piano. There is too much of a crowd for me to know which of these men is Mosake. I turn to leave, when a hand on my shoulder stops me.

"So you managed to get off that truck without too much loss of blood."

This is not the fat man who yelled at me, so it must be Mosake. He speaks in a low, gravelly voice, as if his words come from somewhere deep in his chest. He's dressed in black and wears a gold watch with a thick leather strap on his right arm and a heavy gold chain around his neck. A soft hat lies at an angle on his head, covering most of his black hair. He smells of tobacco, new leather, and after-shave. He's taller than I am, and he grips my shoulder hard. I can feel the strength in his arms. I mumble and shake off his hand. Nobody touches me.

"You've come for my audition?" He is smiling, but I notice that his eyes are not. It's a thin smile for such a wide mouth, and it doesn't seem to fit among the solid features of his face.

I don't know what he's talking about, but it sounds like a challenge.

"Yes," I say.

"Go to the toilet and clean up. We're starting now. Cathy, take him."

He gestures to a pretty woman in a yellow dress who is sitting at a table. She comes over to me, and before I can say anything she leads me away, past Mosake's fat passenger. He calls over to Mosake and jerks his thumb at me.

"Mosake, you can't be serious. Not that terrorist!"

I want to punch him in his big fat face. His shirt is bright orange, and his belly bulges out between his buttons and hangs over his belt. He eats too much. I don't like him.

"You worry about the money, Oswald, and I'll worry about the talent," Mosake says, leaving me to Cathy. She wears makeup on her eyes and lips. I think the jewelry she wears around her neck must be very expensive. She has dark red fingernails. This is not a township woman, but a lady from the city.

"What's your name?" she asks.

"Seraki."

"Well, Seraki, have you ever auditioned before?" She smiles.

I look away briefly, wondering if I should lie, but I like looking at her face. She has a nice smile. It shows her teeth and it makes you want to grin back at her. "No," I mumble.

"It doesn't matter. It's very easy. Mosake will tell you what to do and then just do what everyone else does. Where do you live?"

"Near here."

"I see," she says. "Your first audition can be frightening. Go in there and clean that blood off your arm. You'll want to look as good as you can."

She points to the door and leaves me.

I go into the toilet and look around. There is an open window and an empty yard outside. I could get out through this window easily. I don't have to stay. I look in the mirror. My face seems small and stupid compared to Mosake's. I have thin lips, a flat nose, a scab on my forehead from a street fight, and small eyes. Mosake's face is strong, defined, and handsome, while mine is weak, childish, and dirty. I don't belong here. I could climb through this window, run across the yard, and be gone. Nobody would miss me. I stand on the toilet seat . . .

Then I hear the piano again in the other room. This time there is singing. It's still loud and it's a tune I don't know. I step down off the toilet and listen with my ear to the door.

It's the sound of an open veld, of clouds racing across the sky, and of the wind chasing through long grass. The girls' voices rise high above the boys', and then the melody changes and the singers begin clapping and stamping. Now the sound is of Friday afternoon at the train station: hooting, shouting, running feet, and sirens. These are songs I don't know, but the music is familiar and it gets to me and I like what I hear.

I consider the open window again. Then I hurry to wash the dust from my face and clean up my arm. There is no reason not to stay and listen to the music. This window will be here later.

The main room is now full of boys and girls standing nervously around the piano, or singing in a small group in the center of the floor. The walls are lined with parents who sit on battered chairs.

One girl stands out from the rest, although she's right there with the others, leaning against the piano. She doesn't seem nervous. She is beautiful. A tiny smile hides in the corners of her mouth as she watches the group singing in the middle of the room. She looks older than the others, but it could be her smart clothes and the makeup she's wearing. Her hair is strung into braids with bright beads that hang around her face and move with her as she sways

10

to the music. Looking at her, I'm glad I didn't climb out the window.

At the far end of the room Mosake is sitting with his hands loosely clasped on the table before him. He's watching the singers closely. His fat friend—Oswald—is chewing on a pencil and making comments out of the corner of his mouth. Cathy's standing behind them. Every now and then she bends forward, places her hand on Mosake's arm, and whispers in his ear. He doesn't answer either of them. His concentration is on the group of young people singing in front of him.

Even at one end of the room he is at the center of everyone's attention. Everyone is singing for him. He watches, without smiling or frowning; he doesn't seem to know that he is at the center. For some time he studies the singers without moving, and then his head turns and his gaze shifts sideways and falls on me.

We stare at each other. I'm not afraid of him. I didn't climb out the window.

He points at me and then at the singers in the center of the room. I nod and walk over to the group, who move aside to allow me among them. Oswald sucks on his pencil, jots something down, and murmurs to Mosake. I ignore them and start singing.

It's easier than I'd expected; the other singers cover my mistakes. I become part of the sound of Friday afternoon, and feel my voice disappear into the other voices, feel my head fill with notes I've never sung before. Soon I begin to hear my own sound among the others and am surprised that although I sing with them, my voice sounds separate.

We're told to sing the first song again, and now I sing louder, hearing the melody of the open veld, racing with the wind through the tall grass, riding the white clouds, and adding my own harmony.

"That's enough," Mosake says, and stands up.

Everyone stops singing.

"Now dance for me!"

No one moves, except to glance at one another.

"Come on. Dancing is part of this."

Behind me, a boy and a girl giggle nervously. Our feet seem nailed to the floor. The boys look helplessly down at their feet. The girls stare blankly at Mosake. Someone at the back asks if we couldn't have some music to dance to.

"Later you'll have music," he says. "Now I want to see what kind of young people I have before me. Dance to your own music."

I think of the skinned cat, the dead man, my father, and my brother, Phakane. I begin to sway from side to side, softly chanting a song I know:

> The sorrow that is Soweto.
> Dark clouds gather over you.
> When will the rains come,
> to wash our sorrow away?

I shift my feet and dance alone—until another boy joins me and we sing and dance together. We lift our voices and grow stronger, and when I raise my fist above my head, a third and then a fourth boy pick up our beat, and then all of us are moving from side to side, singing, stamping our feet, and filling the room with our voices. I feel my anger turn to joy as we chant and bounce to the rhythm of the *toyi-toyi* dance. One foot up, the other a hop, down again, up again, one foot up, the other a hop, down again, up again . . .

"Stop!"

Everyone goes tense around me. In silence we wait while Mosake talks to Cathy and Oswald. Then he jabs his finger at a short girl in front—"Out!"—and one of the boys standing beside me—"You, next to the terrorist! Out!"

The girl moves to the side where her mother puts her arms around her and leads her toward the door. The boy mutters a curse and then walks proudly out of the room alone. Everyone else is shuffling about, trying not to be at the end of Mosake's finger.

"What is he doing?" I whisper to the boy next to me.

"Shhh, it could be you next."

"Back to the piano, Josh," Mosake calls across the room to a man dressed in a white shirt who is hunched over the piano. Josh raises his hands above the piano and with a flourish strikes the keys. We listen to the opening bars of a familiar song and all around me people breathe sighs of relief before we start singing again. Our voices join in this comfortable melody, but from somewhere at the back a girl's voice rings out clearly above the rest.

She might be the same girl who gave me that dirty look, which now seems like ages ago. But singing, she looks sweet and pure like her notes, and her eyes are far away in the music. Her skin and hair are as soft and warm as her voice. She's not the beautiful one—that one is still standing by Josh at the piano. This girl has a delicate face, with a small nose and high cheekbones. She has a determined look in her eyes, which shine brightly as she sings.

I smile at her, but she doesn't see me. She is looking only at Mosake. She seems in awe of him.

"Who is singing the soprano line?" Mosake interrupts.

Josh stops playing and turns around. I didn't really notice Josh carefully before, or the big, chunky rings on his long, thin fingers. He has an earring and there is a light sheen of sweat over his face. He seems too thin to be playing the piano so loudly.

"Who was singing this line?" Josh asks, as he turns away to play the melody.

Nobody moves. We wait.

"Come on my little songbird, Daddy's not going to bite!" he says, winking at us.

The girl pushes through the group. "It was me," she says timidly.

"Name?" Mosake asks.

"Nongeni."

"Let's hear you by yourself."

Josh plays and Nongeni sings. It's like honey pouring from a spoon, like dust floating in the sunshine, like rain dripping on leaves. The beautiful girl beside the piano doesn't seem to be enjoying the song. Cathy leans over Mosake and whispers longer this time, but he doesn't look at her, and Oswald continues to tap his fat nose with his pencil.

Nongeni stops singing. The air is filled with the memory of her sound.

"Thank you," is all Mosake says.

Nongeni turns around and rejoins the group. Her eyes are bright with triumph. She looks stronger now, not as delicate as I first thought. We make room for her as if she has been touched by magic. The moment passes, and we continue to dance and sing until our clothes are soaked with sweat.

"You, out," Mosake's finger points again. "And you, too. You may leave now."

It is getting later, and there are only twenty of us left, as Mosake sits at his table, cool, aloof, watching, instructing, and never changing his expression or his tone of voice. Then he lifts his chin to speak, and the room grows quiet by silent command.

"You, out! And you! Out!"

They pick up their bags and go. Some of the parents mutter angrily. He takes no notice, concentrating only on those of us who are left. And then he says "Take five."

I look questioningly at the boy beside me and he whispers, "It's a five-minute break." We mill about the room; no one talks to anyone else, except Josh who joins the other three at the table.

I like the power Mosake has—it's swift and fierce. He only has to point his finger. He will not point his finger at me. I did not climb through that window, and now, with only eighteen of us left, I feel like I'm clinging to that high-speed truck again. Only this time it's not a truck and I'm not worried about how to get off. This time I'm loving the thrill and the danger of holding on, of not knowing where I'm going. It is the same feeling as before, only more so.

Once when I was visiting my uncle in the mountains, he took me to a cave. We climbed for hours until he led me deep inside the rock, and we stood in the dark as he explained how this was a cave that could sing. Then, in his deepest voice, he called out, "Sing with me, Seraki," and we sang—my uncle, the cave, and I. Our voices joined the voices of the walls and the darkness around us, and bounced backward and forward, in and out of our mouths, and all the way through us into our bones and our blood.

We laughed together and sang some more, and I feel just like that now. This music has a place for me within it, like all the times my brother would come home from work and call me funny names and put his arms around me and pretend to squeeze me to death. He would hold me so tight I could not get away and I would struggle, but not too hard, because I didn't want to get away. This room is not my uncle's cave, and Mosake is not Phakane—and yet I feel the same here.

Slowly, Mosake rises, stretches, and walks to the front of his table. For a big man he moves gracefully, without ever seeming hurried. He leans lightly against the table, folds his arms, and nods as if he is thinking something of great importance. His movements are defined, strong. His face shows no emotion, yet his dark eyes draw us to him. When he speaks it is as if he is talking to each one of us alone.

"Right, that's it! You eighteen have been chosen. You are what I want."

Some of the boys shout, some of the girls shriek with excitement, two boys slap hands with each other, girls are hugging one another. Nongeni clenches her fist and strikes the air over and over again. I do nothing. What does he mean that we are chosen?

"Come over here, now. Parents, you also." He waits while all the people in the room move in closer. "I'm going to say this once only," and he waits again. I take a place at his feet and my eyes are drawn to Cathy, who is smiling down at me from the table. She seems pleased at something I've done. I smile back at her.

"Of course you are still the queen of song, Gloria." Josh's voice fills the space between Mosake's words. The beautiful girl—Gloria, I now find out—is talking angrily to Josh, who's patting her arm and saying, "I promise, Baby, I promise." He winks at Mosake and his laugh is like a car backfiring. He looks even thinner standing up, and he waves his hands around as if he's catching flies while he calms Gloria down.

15

Mosake fires a glance at them both. Josh blows Mosake a kiss, slaps himself on the wrist, and whispers something into Gloria's ear. She laughs loudly, and Josh quickly clamps her mouth with his hand, looking apologetically in Mosake's direction.

"We'll start rehearsals next Monday," Mosake begins. "We'll work every afternoon during the week and all day Saturdays. No one is to use this production as an excuse to miss school," he adds, looking straight at me. "You'll all be paid seven rand a rehearsal and ten rand a performance. The performances will be held at the new community center, the one with a proper stage."

Seven rand a rehearsal and ten rand a performance! We're to be paid for dancing and singing? It's crazy! I'm going to be paid money for doing the *toyi-toyi!* Mr. Nzule will never believe me. He'll say I stole the money. Seven rand a rehearsal and ten rand a performance! It's a fortune!

". . . misses one rehearsal will be out of the production." It's fat Oswald speaking now.

Then someone asks a question. "How many weeks rehearsing and how many performances?" It is a man in a gray suit, one of the parents.

"There will be six and a half weeks of rehearsal and two weeks of performances. We open on the seventeenth of September—in time for spring."

I struggle to work it out. Six days a week, times seven rand, times six and a half weeks, plus ten rand for twelve performances.

Three hundred and ninety-three rand!

I'm rich! I dropped off a truck, spotted a sports car, sang a song, danced a dance—and suddenly I've got lots of money! Almost four hundred rand!

"You're paying less than the minimum wage for children. You know that, don't you, Mr. Mosake?" the man in the gray suit continues.

"If you don't like the terms, I suggest you take your child and go. Now!" Mosake replies.

Nongeni is shaking her head furiously at the man in the gray suit. He must be her father. He hesitates, considers his daughter's eyes, which sparkle with tears, and says nothing further.

"Any other questions?" Mosake asks the adults.

They stir and look at one another, but nobody says anything more.

Cathy starts handing out forms for us to fill in. When she reaches me she says, "You must get your parents to sign," and she points to a space on a line. "And then bring it back to me."

Mosake turns his back to us and begins to gather up his papers from the table. As he opens his briefcase he says, "You understand that I expect perfect attendance and one hundred percent effort at all times. Anyone who thinks they can get away with giving less had better leave now." He continues to pack his case.

Nobody moves. The room is silent except for the rustling of his papers.

"Good! Then we are all in agreement. I will see you all on Monday straight after school. My rehearsals start promptly. Don't be late." He turns, looks us over one last time, and leaves the room.

Oswald takes his pencil from his mouth, twists it around, and then puts it behind his ear. He scratches his enormous belly, farts, and pats his fat cheeks. He looks at us doubtfully, shakes his head, and follows Mosake to the door.

"Old Pork Chops can't stand to see us making any money," the boy next to me says, gesturing toward Oswald's back. "To him we're just a mountain of rands and cents thrown away."

"Who is he?"

"Financial backer of the show. Thinks he's pretty smart, but his real money comes from selling illegal booze to shebeen queens who run speakeasies," he says, laughing.

"Hey, Teddy boy, so you made it. How much money did your old man give Mosake to get you in?" A tall boy saunters over to congratulate the boy I'm talking to. Teddy punches him on the shoulder.

"Sipho, I'm surprised to see a *skelem* like you amongst us elite."

They slap hands, joke loudly, and act like men. I'd like to join them, but I wouldn't know what to say. I move away. Nobody knows me and that's the way I want to keep it. There's too much money involved.

"We have to clear out now," Josh says as he locks the piano and pulls a cloth over it. "The women's sewing circle comes in here next, bless their stitching souls." He turns and looks at me. "Ever been on a rocket ship before?"

I shake my head.

"Well, welcome aboard. It can be a bumpy ride in places, but that's showbiz! You're on your way to the moon."

I still don't know what he is talking about. Mosake is gone and somehow the room looks ordinary, as if nothing important has happened here. Whatever it was, it is over. I'm standing alone in an empty room, holding a piece of paper.

I go to the door and look outside. The adults are standing by their cars calling to their children. The world outside this room looks ordinary too. Nothing's changed. The evening cooking fires have been lit, and the haze of smoke is beginning to collect over the township, dimming the street lamps and the lights of cars. The roads are busy with commuters from the city, carrying their weekly pay packets and filling the air with dust. The Naughty Boys and the shebeen queens are out there, too, waiting to get their share of other people's money. It's Friday night just like any other Friday night, but for me it's different.

Today something important happened to me. Today I got a job, and on coming Friday nights I will also have money in my pockets. Now I've got to get home. It's a long way, but I don't mind. I've got lots to think about—like how am I going to spend all that money? Can I use it to help Phakane? How am I going to explain all this to Mr. Nzule? Can I make him believe me when I almost can't believe me myself? Will I really get paid to sing and dance? Of course it's true. I have this paper to prove it.

For the first time I actually look at the paper. Then I fold it carefully and slip it into my pocket. No, it's too valuable for my pocket. I take it out and push it down the front of my shirt. I like the way it feels there, next to my skin. It's my proof. I won't tell Mr. Nzule anything about it. I'll make my mother sign for me and promise not to tell him. If she won't I'll sign it myself.

When I have the money I'll tell Mr. Nzule. Then he'll have to believe me. He'll pay attention to what I'm doing and won't just say it's a way to keep me off the streets. He never thinks of me except in ways of keeping me off the streets. Lots of people are saying that these days. Keep them off the streets.

I run home.

UNCLE, DO IT

On Friday nights people in Soweto walk quickly, glancing over their shoulders, and scuttle into their homes, feeling safe behind locked doors and net curtains. Tonight, dogs are barking too. They can smell the danger.

The Naughty Boys are out on the streets tonight. It's late and if my mother's at home, she will be worried. I'm too tired to run any more, and the cuts on my leg are pounding as I walk home. My bloodied arm has dried into a thick, black scab. A woman, loaded down with her shopping, sees my wounds and looks at me nervously. She rushes past me and into her house. I can hear her locking the door. She knows the Naughty Boys are on the streets tonight. Everyone knows that.

They are nowhere in sight, but somewhere they gather to sharpen their knives and plan their evening's chaos. Shebeen smoke, sorghum beer, and pay packets are everywhere on Friday nights. With no sign of police vans or army trucks, it's a green light for the Naughty Boys.

They laugh at net curtains and locked doors. If they want you, they throw a petrol bomb through your window. Then they wait until there's enough flames, enough smoke, and you come rushing out. After that they've got you, and maybe it would've been wiser to stay inside with the fire and smoke.

They did it to our next-door neighbor, Mr. Thilani, who used to sit outside his back door on Saturday afternoons listening to soccer matches on the radio. I was still in primary school then and I didn't know the things I know now. I liked to listen to the soccer, too, and Mr. Thilani had his radio on so loud that everyone could listen, until his wife would shout at him to turn it down.

No one would say out loud that the Naughty Boys did it, but the night they threw the petrol bomb into the window through Mrs. Thilani's handmade curtains, there was much screaming. Mr. Nzule, Mother, Phakane, and I ran out of our house, but when Mr. Nzule saw what was happening he made us go back inside. Even though I was only there for a moment, I remember the smoking house, the smell of burnt plastic, faces lit by the fire, and the screams. They did not sound human, but like a big, broken machine with rotor blades scraping against iron bolts. I didn't know a person could make a noise like that.

My brother would not be sent home. He pushed past Mr. Nzule and ran to the crowd at Mr. Thilani's front door. He was too late. Mr. Thilani was dead and the Naughty Boys had scattered. When the police came they took my brother with them. I suppose they thought he was one of the Naughty Boys. The following day when he came back, he had purple bruises on his face. He said the police had beaten him, and I was sad for Phakane and glad I was still young.

That was the year of the troubles—1986—when there were many more fires, and I didn't understand a lot of what was happening. Now there's mostly only smoke.

But my brother explained everything to me on our way back from our neighbor's funeral. He said that Mr. Thilani was killed because he'd been seen talking to the police, and going to work for the Sowetan council.

Mr. Nzule said Mr. Thilani didn't have the right *muti* and it was easy for the Naughty Boys to smell out a house not protected. Mr. Nzule buys our *muti* from the old *sangoma* who lives in the rubbish dump. He thinks the bags of dust and potions will stop anything from harming our house. I believe it and I don't believe it. It's a hard thing to think about clearly, because it's been around for so long.

Muti helped and didn't help my mother in 1986.

In those times, my mother was stopped on the road by the Naughty Boys on her way home from work. They said she mustn't go to her job. Going to work was against their orders. They said people who went to work were supporting the system of Apartheid. They forced her to eat the soap powder she had bought from a white man's shop. She was sick for a long time after that. Then Mr. Nzule got special traveling *muti* to protect my mother on her way to work. After that nobody bothered her again when she wore the pouch of rat's bones, redwood root, and chicken-shit powder. *Muti* is like that: It works and it doesn't work.

Now I am older and I know enough to keep to the shadows. I don't want to be seen by that circle of men there under the street lamp. They are too relaxed, too casual, as three of them crouch on their haunches in the shaft of the lamplight, and two more stand watching, smoking, leaning over the edges of the light. They are playing betting dice. They are Naughty Boys.

But a part of me wants to go over to them, light up a cigarette, scoop up the dice, and shout "Lucky sixes, tricks or nixes" or "Snake eyes come to daddy-do" with them. They are strong, safe, super cool, unbeatable. I wonder what "Dirty threes, on your knees" means?

Here on this deserted street, late at night, nobody can touch them, because they are throwing their dice and shouting their secret words to one another. I can't help but stare at them, and I know that stopping here is a stupid thing to do. They will notice me, and then one of them does.

"Get out of here, boy," he growls.

The Naughty Boys own the street. The men with the dice don't even look up. They are shaking the white bones, spitting into their palms, shouting their oaths: "Cats eyes, stay alive!"

The skinned cat. Is someone going to die tonight? I turn and run down the street, but not because I'm afraid. I run the rest of the way home because I'm not stupid.

As I turn the last corner I hear the brassy, hip-hop wail of a saxophone. The sound is definitely coming from my alley, and people out here on the street have stopped to listen. I'm proud that they are listening and peering toward my house. They are looking at one another and wondering what is happening. I know what is happening even though I have not been home yet. The sound of the saxophone can mean only one thing. I run down the alley and into the music that is getting louder to welcome me home.

All the lamps are lit, and from the alley I hear clapping and singing coming from inside. When I reach the door, I stop and wait, holding tight to the latch. I want to listen to the music, and picture my mother's brother, before I actually go in. Once I open the door, the music and the people will spill all over me and everything will get complicated and maybe not be so nice as it is right now.

But I can wait no longer. I open the door, and there he is. Uncle. He stands in the middle of the room, playing his saxophone, dancing around my mother. He is turning around and around her, and she is protesting and laughing while he is playing and shouting, "Dance, *sisi*, dance!"

My home has changed. The table and boxes have been pushed against the walls to clear a space for their dancing. My home is crowded with people standing in a circle clapping their hands: Mrs. Mcebi and her daughters, Gladys and Rosie, the next-door neighbors; and some people I don't know. I have never seen so many people in our shack before. My uncle has still not seen me, but he will. Oh yes, he will, and then I'll run into his arms. My uncle is here! Everything changes when my uncle is here.

"*Mshana,* my sister's son, Seraki!" he shouts. "Make room for my *mshana.*"

He passes the saxophone to my mother, opens his arms to me, and I see only him. He is the same as I pictured him at the door, the same as I remember when I was in the country. Just as strong, as tall, as funny as I remember him. I don't want to dance. I want to stand in the middle of the room and look at him in his bright parrot shirt, pin-striped slacks, one-hundred-rand pair of Ace shoes, but he is dancing and he makes me want to do the same. We slap our ankles, slap our knees, jump and kick, and slap our thighs. It's the dance the miners do at the gold mines and everyone is laughing, clapping, and singing. Even my mother.

She is passing out cool drinks to everybody and complaining about the mess. She pretends to be bothered about the noise, the laughter, and the confusion, but she is excited. She gets like this when her brother is here. Sometimes when my uncle comes, it is hard for me to recognize her as my mother.

"My brother is turning our house into a shebeen." She laughs to her guests. "Soon the police will be here to take us all to Vorster Square." She complains, but I can see how pleased she is.

"Better to dance now, then, before they come, *sisi,*" Uncle shouts, and he picks up his saxophone again and makes it sing along with the music.

"No, Vula, that's enough!" But my mother is drowned out by the laughing, the dancing, and her brother's saxophone.

Later, the people leave, the music is turned off, and my mother busies herself with putting the house back the way it always is. Mr. Nzule comes home. He greets Uncle with a nod of his head. Mr. Nzule does not sit down. I can tell he is not pleased to see him.

"How long are you staying?" he asks, and I see my mother's eyes flash in anger, but she says nothing.

"I don't know. As long as I am needed. Sit here, Seraki, sit by me," my uncle answers with a grin. Mr. Nzule makes a grunting noise, stares hard at my mother, and leaves. He does not look at me. He would not dare to look at me in front of my uncle. He knows the tradition and he must uphold it. My brother and I are the responsibility of our uncle. Mr. Nzule's power lies over his sisters' sons, but Mr. Nzule has no sisters.

"Some things never change, hey *sisi*?" my uncle says quietly from his seat at the table. My mother is serving him tea and fussing over him, and checking out the window for Mr. Nzule. She knows Mr. Nzule will make her pay for this incident. She knows but hides this from Uncle.

"Pay no attention to Nzule," she says, watching her husband walk away down the alley. "These are difficult times and he does not mean to be rude."

Why is she saying this? She's wrong. Mr. Nzule always says what he means. He never tries to be anything other than what he is. Except with his pretty women.

My mother closes the door and locks it before she returns to my uncle.

"And you? You did not even have the manners to tell me you were coming," she says, pouring him more tea and pushing a plate of biscuits in front of him. I wish she would stop all this clearing up from the party and sit down and join us.

"A surprise is no surprise if you know it before, *sisi*," he says, winking at me.

"Tell me about our family. Is Father well?"

"I think his time is coming, but he still drinks enough beer to put the young ones to shame."

"And Auntie?"

"Still beating our uncle with her stick and crying about her immoral relatives lost in the city."

They are talking together, and, as I hear news of family I seldom see, I feel warm inside. It is a feeling I only have when my uncle comes to visit us. Right now I am so full with happiness I have nothing to say so I just sip my tea, listen, and wait until my uncle finishes with the biscuits before taking a cream-centered one I've had my eye on.

"Seraki, what have you done to your arm?" my mother finally asks.

"I fell."

She shakes her head and clicks her tongue against her teeth at me as she warms a cloth, cleans my wounds, and dabs red burning stuff on me. Despite the pain, I like the attention I am getting from her and Uncle.

"This looks like more than a fall, *mshana*," he says knowingly when my mother goes outside to fetch more water.

"I caught a ride and jumped off a Pick 'n Pay truck, like the men do," I answer proudly, but Uncle does not laugh as I hoped he would.

"You will be a man sooner than you wish, Seraki," and he reaches across the table for my arm. He squeezes it tightly and says in a serious voice, "There is no rush, *mshana*, believe me."

"And you, my brother, when will you become a man? You're still not working," my mother says, pulling a crate up to the table and finally sitting down.

"Work is hard to find, *sisi*."

"Especially if you're not looking!"

My uncle smiles, bites into another biscuit, and winks again at me.

"Your mother is always the same, Seraki. She is like a record player that is stuck. Every time I come she asks me the same question."

"But, Vula, it's true . . ."

"Now, *sisi*, you know me. I get along. When have you known me not to get along?"

"That's what I worry about. It's good that you do not live here. I would worry more."

I like sitting here with them, being part of their conversation. I look from one to the other as my uncle talks and my mother fusses. I do not want them to see my eyelids grow heavy or the yawn that keeps pulling on my mouth. But my mother notices anyway and she shoos me off to bed.

25

Uncle takes the lamp and directs me across the room by my shoulders. He draws the curtain behind us.

"I followed a red sports car today, Uncle, and did an audition. And I got hired. I'm going to get almost four hundred rand for dancing and singing."

He laughs and takes up the lamp again. "You are dreaming already and you are not even asleep, *mshana*," he says.

"You will be here tomorrow morning?"

"Yes, *mshana*, I will be here."

"You will not leave in the night like you did last time?"

"No, Seraki. I am staying for a while," he says, drawing the curtain and leaving the room.

The primus stove hisses. Chairs scrape the floor, cutlery is washed. I lie in bed listening to my mother and my uncle beyond the curtain. Their voices have dropped as if I'm already asleep. They are talking adult talk.

"You and Nzule, how is he treating you?" my uncle asks.

"The same. No better, no worse."

"And the women?"

"The same, but don't start preaching to me, little brother. I am lucky to have this roof, this bed, and stove."

"You speak like a woman from the country, *sisi*. We are modern here in the city. Those traditions of men with their many wives are for the old times, and you—"

"Vula, I said no preaching! I know what I know, and I must keep what peace there is here."

There is a tea-sipping silence between them, and then my mother asks about his journey, and he tells her, and he asks her about her white madam, and she tells him, and they talk on and on about small things, about meat prices, about rent, about the police, and it seems that they are both taking the long way around before talking about my brother. And then they do.

"And you have heard nothing—they have not told you where they are keeping him?" I hear my uncle ask.

I do not hear my mother's reply. It doesn't matter. I know what it is.

"I have come to help," my uncle says, "to find a way of seeing him, to see if he is well."

"Vula, I don't know anymore, what if he's . . . ?"

I do not hear what she says, but I know what my mother fears. Sometimes when I think very hard about Phakane I am afraid of it too. What if he is dead? We have heard how sometimes people do not come back. They are found dead and reported as suicides. Nobody knows how or why, and nobody asks.

My mother does not talk about my brother in front of me anymore. It's as if he's already dead, but I will not believe that. I try to listen to what they are saying. Now that Uncle is here he will do something, I know he will.

Their conversation is getting softer and softer. I feel my body relax. I don't want to sleep. I want to hear what they are saying about Phakane, who is rolling a tractor tire down the street, shouting for me to hold on. I grip the insides of the tire, as the world goes round and round, up and down. I scream for him to go faster, faster. I feel safe inside the tire with my brother rolling it along the road.

It is too fast now and I want to stop. He always stops when I shout. Stop! Phakane, stop! This time he doesn't. I roll faster, trapped in the tire, shouting for Phakane, as the world spins past. And then I take off from within the tire and start flying. The air rushes past me as I sail high above the earth. From the sky I look for my brother, but Phakane is gone. Far down below I see the tire rolling by itself. He is being pulled away. He grabs my blanket, holds onto it. Men with peaked hats, white faces, drag him away into the dark and I am falling, falling, falling . . .

We are hopping down the street in the sunshine, Uncle and I. We don't care that people look at us. We jump over stones and bricks and broken bottles in the road. I haven't forgotten our game. If you turn over a stone you marry a *sangoma,* and a spell is cast over you for the rest of your life.

It is hard for me to believe how much I used to enjoy this game. Now it feels stale, worn out. When I was younger I was always marrying a *sangoma,* but now I am good enough to stay a bachelor, like Uncle. I think we are playing it because it reminds us of a time when we only had to worry about marrying *sangomas.*

"Uncle, do you still believe in the power of witches?"

"There are things more evil than those women, Seraki, but they help some people to think that life is different and simpler than it really is. Some people do a good job of disguising reality with potions and magic spells," Uncle says, and I know he is talking about Mr. Nzule.

"And *muti?*"

"*Muti* is as strong as you want it to be, Seraki," he says. "Everything can become *muti:* stones, trees, a lucky penny, dogs, cats, a girlfriend, grandparents, thunder, even God. Everything."

"Everything?"

"Everything that we put faith in. But *muti* can also be dangerous. You must never let it control you. You must always be the one in control."

My uncle is like that: He makes sense come easy.

After a while I stop hopping and walk properly until Uncle looks back at me and stops too. I want to talk about other things.

"Last night, Uncle, I heard you talking to my mother. You said you were going to help us find Phakane. What are you going to do that Mr. Nzule has not already done?"

"Why do you call your father mister, Seraki?"

"He wants respect. I'll show him respect."

"Is that all? There is another reason, not so?"

How can I make Uncle understand that I don't think of Mr. Nzule as a real father? Not anymore.

"Uncle, what are you going to do that he hasn't already done?"

Uncle does not answer straight away. He looks at me. I don't meet his eyes. I don't want to talk about Mr. Nzule. I want to talk about my brother.

"I shall track him down and go to where they are keeping him and ask to see him. Sometimes they can be reasonable, and if they are not, I will pester them until they get tired of me. I will find Phakane."

He speaks so firmly that I believe him, even though I know it is impossible. I believe in what my uncle says. He is strong and clever. They will listen to him and do what he says.

"And then you will get him out?"

"That I cannot say, but I will try."

"Uncle, do it. Do it and get him out."

He stops walking, turns me toward him, and holds me by the shoulders. He looks deep into my eyes. He knows how much I think about Phakane, how much I miss him, and that I worry too. He knows everything about me and everything I feel. I can see my worry in his eyes.

"I can only do what I can do. Nothing more, Seraki. You must understand that."

I nod, but I do not turn away from his face.

"Tell me about this audition, and about this red sports car . . ."

Now we are talking easily again, as if Phakane and everything about him has flown away for the moment. I let Uncle drag the details out of me. At first he laughs and teases. He thinks I'm making it up. And then he believes me, so I tell him all about what happened yesterday, but in the back of my head I can't stop thinking about Phakane.

Do it, Uncle. Do it.

ISEZELA

I hate firsts of anything: the first day at school, the first date with a girlfriend, and meeting first-time visitors to our home. I always feel so tense, raw really, and everything I say seems thick and clumsy. It's like walking with my hands outstretched in a dark room, my shins waiting to be knocked. I hate polite talk, too, talking for talking's sake, about the weather, or programs on television, or the cheapest soap for sale at the supermarket. And while everyone is talking politely, I become quiet because I have nothing to say to people I don't know. My words seem to hang on a clothesline, pegged up and dripping wet. Why isn't it all right to just be quiet? It should be, but of course it isn't. Whenever I meet people for the first time they must think I'm rude or angry because I don't talk like they do.

I hate firsts, and I do my best to avoid them. But mostly I can't and this is what I'm thinking as I walk up to the hall for the first rehearsal of Mosake's musical on Monday afternoon after school.

I'm disappointed that the red sports car isn't parked out front of the community center. It was one of the reasons I came back. Teddy walks past, looks me up and down, and heads into the building without saying a word. Maybe he hates polite talk as much as I do. Several girls walk aimlessly around, ignoring everybody. I hate it when kids play cool. It gives you no choice but to play cool too. So that's what I do, even though I recognize some of them from Friday, and I know they know I recognize them.

I follow Teddy inside and stand, my back and one foot up against the wall, waiting for something to happen. I'm trying to look like I don't really care if nothing happens at all, as if I'm standing here by chance, enjoying the view. It's just this sort of stupid thing that "firsts" make me do. Cathy is collecting the forms we were told to bring, and I quickly slip mine into her pile. I don't want her to check my signature too carefully.

Two girls are talking a little ways off to the left of me. I pretend not to listen to them, but I listen anyway. One is Nongeni, the girl with the beautiful voice and the well-dressed father. She's looking quite smart again today, in crisp new denims and a fancy blouse. Everyone else is wearing their stupid school uniforms.

"And then he kicked her out and she never got to do opening night," she says to her friend, who is a lot bigger than Nongeni. The girl looks tough; she's got thick legs and strong arms. She has shaved her hair very short, and wears no makeup.

"I've heard he can be very strict."

30

"Well, he has to be, Tisha. That's what it means to be a professional," Nongeni says.

"Don't tell me she's a professional! Who is she?" Tisha says, indicating someone across the room.

I glance over to where they are looking and all three of us are staring at the beautiful girl who stood by the piano through the whole audition. I listen carefully to the answer.

"That's Gloria, Mosake's star. I thought you knew her, Tisha. She's always his female lead," Nongeni says.

"Her nose is as big as two thumbs," Tisha says.

"I'll bet the three of us are the only ones here who have ever been in a show before."

"What makes you say that?"

"Look at the way they're hanging around. They think it's going to be one big party. They haven't a clue what it'll be like, let alone working with Mosake."

The girls notice me listening to them, so I push away from the wall to look for another place to stand. I am having that "firsts" feeling again.

Mosake comes into the room and goes straight to his table. He is dressed in black again, with his soft hat in place on his head. He takes off his dark glasses, flips open his briefcase, and looks about the room. The chatter dies as Josh takes his place at the piano. Cathy is standing a little to one side with Gloria. Everyone silently watches Mosake, waiting for him to speak.

Carefully he removes the papers from his case and arranges them on the table beside a brown paper bag. He closes his briefcase, snaps the latches, and looks up. His eyes scan the room, and then he smiles and laughs out loud.

"It's nice to see you all here today. We're ready to begin and you are all perfect! All of you, except"— I follow his finger— "you over there." He's pointing to Nongeni. "This isn't a fashion show, young lady. We're here to work."

Nongeni slips behind Tisha and drops her head.

"Right. Now let's come together and talk about why we are here and what we are going to do."

31

I let the others close in ahead of me. I don't want to be the first to move. I want to stay at the back. When we are settled in an arc at his feet, we sit and wait and watch as his left hand digs deep into the brown paper bag.

When his hand slowly comes into view again he is holding a small crocodile. Its head is raised and twisted slightly to one side. Red gleams from the depths of its eye sockets, and its tail is tensed, ready to lash out. A sudden hiss comes from its open jaws.

Our eyes dart to one another. Nobody knows what's going on. I stare, fascinated by the darkly bronzed beast in Mosake's hand. I think of a lizard flicking its tongue, a snake ready to strike, and then of danger. Nothing specific. It's just a shiver, a glimpse, a smell of something threatening.

We fidget, some of us stand up, others shuffle away as Mosake tosses the crocodile into the air. It rises high above our heads, writhing, twisting, flickering with a shimmer of gold-reflected light. The crocodile seems to hover beneath the ceiling, staring down at us, waiting as we giggle nervously, scream, and scurry to safety. My back is pressed against a side wall. My eyes follow the crocodile down, until it hits the floor and rolls onto its back. It is stiff and still in the center of an empty circle.

Mosake walks over to it, places his expensive shoe on the paleness of its underbelly, and steps down. It squeaks harshly. He raises his foot slightly and then slowly, shifting his weight, presses down on the crocodile again. This time it moans gently. Some of the kids leave the safety of the walls.

Mosake speaks.

"This is a plastic toy, but to all of you here, for a moment at least, it was frighteningly real. It was a monster with the power to startle and confuse you. And why? Because it's the shape of one of our African myths, iSezela—the old, evil crocodile that lies in the shallow water ready to attack the innocent, and drags its victim to the bottom of the murky river to rot. This plastic toy, this representation of a mythic crocodile, threatened you all." He passes the toy in front of us and squeezes it slowly, and then faster and harder, pumping it until it makes a ridiculous hiccuping wheeze, and we are all laughing at it.

"But when you know how to control it, then it is harmless and pathetic," Mosake says, casually offering the crocodile to one of the boys, who instantly stops laughing and takes a step backward.

Mosake shakes his head sadly. "But you see, even when you know that it's a toy, you are still afraid. The myth is even more powerful than you understand. Your fear is irrational. This is a toy crocodile, and yet you are still afraid."

"I'm not afraid," I say, and step toward Mosake.

Everyone stares at me as I hold out my hand for the crocodile. I don't know why I stepped forward, or why my palm is open in front of Mosake.

"Ahh, so there is a challenger among us?" he says, and slowly he moves to pass the crocodile to me, holding it steady over my hand. Then he twitches it suddenly, and instinctively my hand jerks away. A few of the boys laugh; someone taunts me from the back.

But I put my hand out again, and the laughter stops as the toy comes down slowly. When the crocodile touches my hand, I cry out in pain and snatch my hand away. It is bleeding. Blood oozes from the center of my palm, and the crocodile is again lying motionless on the floor. Startled, the others step back, away from the magic of the bronzed, plastic crocodile that bites.

"And yet it still can harm you. Somehow, impossibly, it can still draw blood. You know it can't—it is only a toy, after all—and yet somehow it does." Mosake kneels down and silently rises with the crocodile, until finally he is upright and holding it high above our heads. "Our country is filled with plastic crocodiles: the old traditions that enslave our people, the educational system, the government and its policies, detention without trial, the State of Emergency, and the crime and violence in our townships. When you think of these things, picture this crocodile. It represents them all." Mosake brings his arm down, pauses, looks over us, and then, unexpectedly, smiles.

"This is what our musical is about: the plastic crocodiles that

33

cause our suffering. And you"—he pauses, passes his hand over us all—"you are the young people who have the power to change everything." Mosake smiles again, gently and knowingly.

His words have punched a hole through my head and awakened the beetles and moths that live there. I feel them stirring, scratching. No one has ever spoken so powerfully to me before. I listen in awe to the words that come so easily and so perfectly from him. I forget the pain in my hand, as I feel those numbing creatures fly away through the hole in my head.

Now he is walking among us, resting his hand on each of the girls' shoulders, gently slapping us boys. Once he has finished, we have all been claimed by his touch.

"We shall call our musical *iSezela*, after the old evil crocodile that terrorized villagers in the time before the settlers came to our land, and which was finally killed by King Shaka and his warriors. *iSezela* will be our musical revelation! *iSezela* will be our cry! *Sezela!*" he shouts, and we all join in and chant with him, *"iSezela, iSezela, iSezela!"*

Mosake walks back to the table and places the crocodile carefully on the edge. We settle down and move closer to the table. I keep a wary eye on the crocodile.

"Let me see where the crocodile bit you," whispers the tall, grinning boy the others call Sipho-Smiler. He's wearing an expensive watch with a silver strap. Twice already I could have pinched it without his noticing, but his school uniform is two sizes too small for him and he has no shoes. That watch must mean a lot to him.

"Is there any blood?" asks Teddy, grabbing my arm. I shake him off and hide my hand in my pocket. Mosake speaks again.

"I'll let our little friend rest here, on the end of the table. Anyone who misbehaves shall be fed to him." He is smiling, but I don't think he is joking. The crocodile gapes hungrily; a row of small teeth runs the length of each jaw. It watches us.

I wonder if the other kids know what Mosake's talking about. I do. I know the crocodile is real. It's beaten Mr. Nzule, and captured my brother, who's right now rotting in its lair. It prowls through the township at night skinning cats and throwing petrol bombs through lace curtains.

"Right! Let's begin!" Mosake says. "Josh, get your nose out of your score. It's time we worked." He gestures toward the piano. "This is Josh. He's our pianist and he'll teach you my songs." Josh does a little bow at the piano, one hand over his heart. As he bows he winks at us.

"Come into my kingdom, you lovely angels, and let Uncle Josh teach you the secrets of music." His voice is sweet, like a woman's, but when he turns and plays the piano he changes completely.

We shuffle into a group around the piano, and as we listen I watch the rings on Josh's fingers flash across the keys, his pelvis thrust into the piano, his feet stamp out the beat, and his head move in time with the music.

Once Josh finishes playing, we all applaud.

"No, no—now is not the time for applause, but for work!" He strikes a chord and sings a line.

We stand mute, nervous. It's another first. He sings the line again.

"Well, what are you waiting for, my little songbirds? I want you to work those muscles in your throats for Uncle Josh."

He sings the line again and cocks his head at us. I swallow hard, and sing after him. By the second line, the others join in. We sing the song over and over again. It's begun. We're on our way. We are singing and I think of nothing but the song. I move closer to the piano. I like to sing. It frees me. I don't have to think when I'm singing. I just open my mouth and let the sound take care of itself.

"Okay, hang on a minute," Josh says, looking up in my direction. "You over there, at the back. What's your name?"

I duck behind the boy in front of me. I've been singing too loudly.

"A little shy, are you?" He waves my shelter aside and points directly at me. "Yes, you! Come here!"

The other kids part, and the empty space between me and the piano seems to suck me through it until I am standing beside Josh.

35

"Sing this for me."

My left leg is shaking, and I can feel the eyes of the others piercing the back of my head. Josh plays a few notes and nods at me. I start to sing. I lose the note. A girl giggles, and gorgeous Gloria looks up sharply from the script she's been reading and winces.

"Relax and sing out, please," Josh says with a smile.

He plays the line again. I do relax and this time I sing even louder until he stops playing the piano and swivels the stool around toward me.

"So, we've got a real voice here! Who'd have thought? Hey, Mosake," he calls across to the table, "were you listening?"

"Of course I was listening," Mosake answers, looking up from his papers. "I knew our terrorist would be okay."

He gets up and comes over to the piano.

"You sing well, boy. Who taught you?"

I feel small beside Mosake.

"Nobody," I mumble to my feet.

"He's a natural. This is raw talent," Josh says, and for some reason it sounds like he's proud.

I'm not proud. I'm squirming, wishing they'd pick on somebody else. So what if I can sing loud. Mr. Nzule always tells me to shut up when I sing loudly. This is stupid. One of the girls is whispering something about my clothes, and I can hear the boys muttering back and forth. I hate being the one to do things first.

After we practice for a while Josh says, "They're ready with this one."

"Good. Then I'll begin."

Mosake organizes us into groups for what he's calling "our opening number." He places me in the middle of the "stage." I'm told to stand on a piece of tape on the floor and when Mosake nods to me, I'm to punch my fist up into the air. The others will come running in from the sides of the room—Mosake is calling the walls "wings"—and everyone will gather around me and repeat my action.

Mosake nods at me. I raise my fist and sing the first line. The cast joins in with a harmony, and then we break as one body into our dance.

My arm is around Gloria, my partner, and we move in time as she smiles up at me. Her eyes are shining. She's beautiful even with those small drops of sweat on her upper lip. She's shaved under her arms. I'm afraid to touch her too close, but I want to feel her body.

"No, that's not good enough. Where's the electricity, where's the fire? Are you afraid of her?"

Mosake is talking to me. I stand dumb, not knowing where to look.

"Seraki, get closer to Gloria, and when you move across the stage, touch her here." Mosake puts my hand on Gloria's thigh. "And then you, Gloria, you do this," and he puts her hand on my chest. "Now move! Hand to chest, hand to thigh. Good! That's it!"

It's all right by me. Some of the girls whistle and some of the boys taunt me, urge me on. Gloria doesn't mind.

The dance is hot, sexy.

Gloria moves closer to me.

I feel her skin, her thighs, her sweet breath.

The others stand around us and clap.

My eyes are locked into Gloria's.

Hand to chest, hand to thigh.

This dance is another first. I've never done anything like this before. Somehow this is different—I may want to touch Gloria's body, but when we do it like this, so carefully, every move worked out, it's more like work than getting off with a girl. Most of the time I don't understand what's going on, but I don't think the others have much of an idea either. When someone makes a mistake, Mosake jokes about it, and we do the number again "from the top." I never know which "top" he means, so I watch Gloria and the others and pretend that it's nothing new to me.

We rehearse all afternoon, stopping only for a ten-minute break. I like doing it over and over again, and now I understand a little of what is actually taking shape. Each time Mosake says "One more time," I know we're not going to do it one, or even two more times, but more like five or six before he's happy.

"Take it from the top . . ."

I run out to center stage and shout the opening lines with my fist in the air. "We're taught what you want to teach us. We learn what you want us to learn. But we cannot live as you want us to live!"

Again, I begin the first song, and the others come running on as before, in twos and threes until the floor is filled. We do it again, and again, all afternoon.

It's dark outside when we finish. Sipho-Smiler calls good-bye to me as he walks off with some of the other boys. I wish they'd asked me to go with them, but I'm glad I know them enough to wave, and I watch them cross the road. Tisha and Nongeni also wave to me as they climb into a fancy car.

Other kids are hanging around, too, like they don't want to go home. I'm glad we're finished. I've got seven rand in my pocket. I can buy some hot chips, some freshly baked bread, and mango chutney—maybe even a Coke. I look at the money, then fold the notes carefully into a small wad and slip them into the leather pouch hanging around my neck.

I'm only waiting around to see the red sports car drive away. Finally Mosake comes out, unlocks the door, and drops into the driver's seat. He revs the engine just like I would do, and in a cloud of dust he swings onto the road and joins the six o'clock traffic. I watch until the car is completely out of sight before I start my long run home.

I pass a café. The bright lights and the smell of frying chips and chicken call me in, but on the corner at the traffic lights, I spot my pal Lucky's LookSmart minibus. If he's in a good mood he might give me a lift. I dash through the traffic and bang on the window. The taxi's already more than full with people wanting to get home, but still the door opens. They can always make space for one more

"Hi, Seraki! What you doing here, bro?"

"Can I have a lift home, Lucky?"

"Get in, bro, get in!" he says.

"I've got no money, but I'll pay you next time," I say.

His passengers groan. The light turns green, and the driver of the car behind leans hard on his horn.

A voice from somewhere in the crush inside the minibus shouts, "Let the snot-nosed *skollie* walk!"

"If you don't like it, *you* can walk," Lucky shouts back.

To me he says, "You can sit on the floor." The door slams shut, Lucky accelerates, and, with a squeal of tires, pulls away.

At home Mr. Nzule is fighting with Uncle. Their words bang on the walls, and clatter against the tin roof before they fall, like stones, cracked and broken on the floor inside. I sit outside, my knees pulled to my chest against the cold. I'm hungry and tired, but I have to wait until they finish this round of hating each other before I dare go in.

"Phakane's trouble is not your business," Mr. Nzule shouts. If my mother was inside they wouldn't be fighting like this. She must be working late, or maybe the train was full . . .

I fiddle with a stick and draw a crocodile in the sand, with its jaws wide open and its teeth too big. This crocodile is trapped in the rectangle of light falling from our kitchen window. It's a crocodile I can rub out whenever I want.

"But he is my business, Nzule. I am his uncle, and his troubles are my troubles. You know that, it's the tradition . . ."

"You only use our traditions when they suit you, Vula. You have never been a proper uncle, and anyway, the old ways are no longer of any use to us now!"

"I don't see you without your *muti*, Nzule."

"That's different, and don't—"

"But let's forget the tradition. Are you too stupid to see that what they do to one of us is all of our business? Isn't it just a matter of sticking together?"

When Ma is around she keeps peace between them. Now the house shakes with their angry voices. I see Mrs. Mcebi part her curtains and look this way.

"I must do what I can to help," Uncle continues. "How can I ignore my sister's family's problems? You want me to pretend my *mshana*'s troubles are not mine?"

"Your kind of help brings pain," Mr. Nzule says bitterly. "You know that, Vula. Your help is dangerous and I don't want it."

Now Mr. Nzule is speaking of the time when I remember him as my father, when Uncle tried to help us with the rent strike. In 1986, the comrades told everyone not to pay their rent to the township council anymore. After that there was big trouble.

I was only twelve then, and I remember lots of funerals, and how we sang and were watched by the police. In the daytime there were street marches and at night, gunfire and fear, and always the stink and smoke of burning tires everywhere.

Uncle was staying with us then, and he had organized a meeting at the Church Hall to protest the rent increases. I remember him trying to convince my parents of how important it was for them to attend. He was angry because my parents stayed at home and wouldn't say anything. They wouldn't even look at him. If Uncle hadn't been there I think they would have paid the extra rent.

But he yelled at them, and explained it to them again and again until they were ashamed. In the end they went to the meeting. Phakane and I went too. Right from the first Phakane agreed with Uncle. He couldn't say so though, not in front of our parents, and maybe that was when his real troubles began.

Now Uncle is angry with Mr. Nzule for speaking about those times again.

"What happened then was not my fault!" he shouts.

"If you had not tried to help . . ."

"Was I to sit and do nothing? All over Soweto people were holding meetings. It wasn't my idea."

"It *was* your idea—"

"But it wasn't my fault that—"

"If you had not tried to help then, the Temba boys would be

40

alive, and I wouldn't have spent six months in a stinking Boer prison!''

I remember how bored I was with all the speeches at the Church Hall. Phakane would not do finger fights with me and he kept shushing me and telling me to listen. He said it was interesting, but after Uncle spoke, there was nothing interesting. Until the lights went out. I thought somebody braver than me was bored, too, and making the meeting into a game.

Then there was the sound of breaking glass and people screaming, and I felt my throat fill with acid, and I couldn't breathe, and my eyes filled with tears so I couldn't see. Everyone was coughing and choking, and the benches were turning over as people ran to the doors.

Phakane held my hand and somehow pulled me out through a broken side window. Together we ran around to the back of the building, and that was when we heard, above the screaming, the first four shots.

Under the streetlights, we could see the police, lined up with their rifles pointed at the back door. They had switched off the lights and broken the windows with their tear gas bombs. And as the people came running out of the building, as Phakane and I watched, we saw the police fire real bullets at them. Esau and Caesar Temba, Phakane's friends, were the first ones we knew who came through the door. They were the first ones we saw collect the bullets.

That meant two more funerals, and more protest meetings and marches, more shots, and more deaths.

After that, when Mr. Nzule agreed and did not pay rent, he got a letter that he didn't understand. Uncle told him to ignore it.

Then they came and took Mr. Nzule away. He spent six months in prison for ignoring the summons. It was the only time I've ever missed Mr. Nzule, but at least we knew where he was. Once a week we saw him and brought him clothes and food. That was when Phakane left school to go to work. I think that was when he met the Union people, who started him in all the other troubles later on.

Uncle stayed the whole time Mr. Nzule was in prison. He went to a lot more meetings, but he never could persuade my mother to go again.

When Mr. Nzule came out of prison Uncle left. It was a good thing, too, because that was when everything started going wrong for Mr. Nzule. He lost his job for being in prison and his friends became suspicious of him. People who are in prison sometimes help the police after they get out. Nobody, not even friends, can be trusted for sure, after they've been in prison.

That was when he started drinking and blaming Uncle for all our troubles. All of that happened in 1986, and now it is a closed subject in our family. We never talk, not ever, about that year.

"So you went to prison for the cause. So you gave something back to the liberation movement. Yes, you have suffered and now it's your elder son. But he has more courage—"

There is a loud crash. I jump up, open the door. My mother's chair is broken on the floor. Mr. Nzule is kicking Uncle, who is cursing, protecting his face, trying to avoid Mr. Nzule's foot. The table is overturned, the plates and cups broken.

"Stop it!" I shout. "Stop it!"

The two men turn and look at me. Then Mr. Nzule shouts at Uncle and tries to kick him again. Uncle pushes past me and tramples my crocodile in the dust.

"Uncle, don't go. Come back," I shout after him down the alley.

"Nzule, you are crazy! No one can talk to you!"

"Uncle!"

"Seraki, come inside! Shut the door! Seraki!"

Mr. Nzule grips my shoulder and pushes me back into the house.

"Your mother's brother is a troublemaker, coming here and living off us without paying anything, turning my wife against me, calling me a coward."

Mr. Nzule is raging. I know better than to say anything. I do not even dare look at him. He will beat me if I do, so I start collecting the knives and forks and broken cups from the floor.

He slams the door. The room is suddenly quiet. I can hear his anger disappear down the alley and Mrs. Mcebi's shouts after him. Whatever his answer is to her, it is lost around the corner. We both know where he's going.

Now I'm glad that my mother's not here. He'd have turned his anger on her, like I do sometimes. It's better that he take it with him to Auntie Somoza's.

NAUGHTY BOYS

I am dreaming that my uncle is shaking my arm and running away down the alley. He is shaking me and running away. I want to wake up, but I feel heavy. In my dream Uncle whispers my name, shakes my arm, and I am awake and staring at his face.

"Seraki, I've found Phakane. Wake up, *mshana*. I've found your brother!"

I can barely hear what he's saying, and wonder why he is whispering. And then I remember the fight with Mr. Nzule, and Uncle storming down the alley, and that it's the middle of the night and everyone is sleeping.

"What?" I am sleepy, still dreaming, trying to wake up.

"Your brother! They are keeping him in Sebokeng Prison. Get out of bed, get dressed," my uncle says, shaking me.

"What time is it?" I say loudly.

"Shhh! I don't want your father to hear."

Uncle tosses my shoes at me and I slip them on. He pulls aside the curtain and walks silently past my parents. Mr. Nzule is snoring. I did not hear him come in last night. I check the luminous hands of my mother's watch on the table. It is 4:50 A.M.

"Hurry, we have a long way to go." Uncle is standing at the door, waiting for me.

I tiptoe past my parents, grab my mother's woolen jersey from the chair, and step outside into the early morning cold. Mist wraps everything in a white blanket. The morning is still, quiet. The warmth of my bed is gone, and I shiver. My uncle puts his arm around me and pushes me forward.

"The place is about two hours from here. We have to take the early morning train into the city and then two taxis to get there. Come, hurry. We are late."

It's not until we are on the train that I fully realize what we are doing: We are going to see my brother.

"How did you find him?" I ask, as we fly through the countryside and an orange glow warms the horizon.

"I went to the police and told them I wasn't leaving until I knew where Phakane Mandindi was being held. I said that if they did not tell me I would go to the Human Rights Commission and get a lawyer for this case. After a long time they told me that he's been transferred to Sebokeng Prison."

My uncle can do anything. It has been almost eight months since we last saw Phakane. Nobody would tell us where he was being detained. We asked at the John Vorster Square headquarters, but they turned us away. It's State of Emergency regulations, they said.

Since the government declared the State of Emergency after the troubles in 1986, anyone can be arrested and detained and the police don't have to give out any information. The police don't even have to say why people are arrested. I wonder if even Phakane knows why he's been detained.

All we were told was that we had to be patient, that he would come home. Nobody had had the courage to demand to see him like Uncle just did. My uncle can do anything.

I sit back and look out the window. The rising sun has turned dew drops on the veld grass into a shimmering gold carpet. And on the horizon, charcoal-smudged clouds hang in an orange and pink sky. Lights flicker on in the houses of the passing towns. The drifting smoke of cooking fires will soon fill the cold air. Mother will be getting up now and fetching the morning water from the communal tap outside, and after the tea is boiled she will call me and wonder where I am before she begins her own long train ride to her madam's house.

"Does Phakane know we are coming?"

"No, it will be a surprise."

I try to imagine my brother, and how he might have changed since last I saw him. I remember him jumping, always running into our house and jumping. Even when we were small he did that, and Uncle called him a springbok who never knows when to stop jumping. I never understood how Phakane always found something to jump about.

He always saw things differently from me. If Mr. Nzule beat us, Phakane would say the pain would be over in an hour. If we had no money until Ma got paid, he would think of all the good things we could buy when she did. When Grandmother died, he said she had gone to a place that was warm, with plenty of food, and where people lived in proper houses. He showed all of this to us by jumping.

The day after he matriculated from school he ran into the house jumping, slapping his knees, and hooting like we'd never seen before. We all looked at him as if he'd gone mad. He didn't stop even when my mother told him to be still. He couldn't be still, and he tried to get me to jump with him. "Come, Seraki. Come jump with the new chairman of the Youth Action Committee," he yelled.

My mother wasn't pleased with his news. He had been a member of the committee since 1986, and like most parents, she felt nervous about anti-Apartheid activities. She told him he would be better off if he stayed out of trouble. But my brother jumped around the room anyway and pulled me off our bed and made me jump with him.

"Things are going to be different now," he said to me. And I believed him. Anyone with enough energy to jump as much as he could, could make things happen.

They came late that night and pounded on our door until even the roof shook. Mr. Nzule stood in the doorway, trying to block their way, but they pushed past him, and then past my mother, who stood in front of the curtain of our room. Then they pulled me off our bed and grabbed Phakane. They dragged my brother from the bed, out the door, and down the alley. Nobody knew why they had come for him, or what Phakane had done. We still don't know.

As we watched, they threw him into their van. It all happened so quickly: One minute he was home, the next he was gone. And the blanket that he and I shared was gone with him. He'd held onto our blanket the whole way. Afterward, my mother bought me a new, softer one, but even so, I liked our bed better the way it was before.

Now it's difficult to picture my brother. I can't imagine him jumping in a prison cell. I try to think of him just standing, but his face doesn't fit on a person standing still.

"Uncle, can people change so much that you don't know them anymore?"

He doesn't answer me. He is looking out the window, lost somewhere in the new day. When I get ready to ask him again he says, "When I play my saxophone, Seraki, the sound is true and beautiful. But if I left it outside in the wind and the rain for a long time, it would get rusted and perhaps even broken. After that, if I played it again, the sound would be terrible. It would no longer be true.

"But the saxophone has not changed. It is still the same one that sounded so beautiful before. I might need to fix the instrument, replace a couple of pads, polish it up again, and treat it with care. Then it will be the same as before. Nothing can change that. It will always be the same saxophone."

Uncle pauses. He is looking hard at me. "Don't think too much about Phakane. He will be as you know him, perhaps thinner, maybe even quieter, but he will always be your brother. Do you understand, *mshana?*"

I nod and turn away to look out the window. I don't know if I believe what my uncle says. My father changed when he came out of prison, and more than just a little bit. He wanted respect, but he stopped working. He wanted love, but he stopped caring. He wanted more money, but then he started drinking. He stopped being my father, and became Mr. Nzule. He's not the person he was before he was taken away. And he was only gone for six months. He wasn't a student when he went away but a man, and now he is a very different man.

Do people know when they are changing? Can they feel it happening? How do I know if I am different from when I was a child? Maybe it's only other people who can see changes, and who notice different things about you. I don't want to notice the things I see now in Mr. Nzule, and thinking about how much he has changed makes me nervous about seeing Phakane.

"He will be the same, you will see," Uncle is saying, but I know it's too complicated to say he will be the same as before, and I think even my uncle is too smart to believe what he is saying himself.

Uncle is fuming. I am too confused and tired now to know what I am feeling. And I have only an hour to get to my afternoon rehearsal.

"Wait till we get home, Seraki. Somebody is going to pay for sending us all this way out here for nothing," Uncle mutters under his breath. "Somebody is going to pay."

We waited outside the prison for five hours. At seven o'clock they said we should come back at ten o'clock. They said the man we had to see was coming into work then. We waited. Then, at ten o'clock, a different man said they would check the prison lists and we waited for another hour. After that my uncle would not tell me what they said. I knew it was not good. By then more people like us had come. We all waited. No one was told anything.

I'm not sure we talked to the right people or asked the right questions. All I know is that we didn't see Phakane.

And I am angry, too, and it's not because we came all this way and it was a useless trip. I'm angry at Uncle and at myself. I want to shout and ask my uncle why he did this to me. Why he made me hope again, after I've gotten used to not hoping and almost not even thinking about Phakane. Now my brother is right up in the front of my brain again.

Dogs run across the floor, circling and snarling at the students. They leap up and bark in their faces. The girls scream, the boys back away, and a policeman swings a *sjambok* above his head. The air swishes with a lash of his long whip and he advances again toward the group.

"You're all *skollies,* terrorists. I should shoot every one of you," he says with a grin on his face. His too-big police hat falls over his eyes. He wiggles the *sjambok* in his hand, slaps the floor with it, and threatens to strike one of the boys. The dogs bark and tug on their leads toward the circle.

I stand outside the circle and wait for my cue. I watch the boys barking like police dogs. They are making it look like a game. Police dogs are more vicious than that, and I have felt the sting of a *sjambok* often enough to know that Sipho-Smiler has no idea how to use one. I would like to run in among the policeman and his dogs and beat them all to the ground. I will show them how it is done. Uncle, why did you make me hope again?

Mosake looks at me. That's my cue. I run into the crowd, push Gloria behind me, and face the dogs and policeman to say my lines.

"We are students, not criminals. We want education, not violence."

The words sound flat. I want to spit into the policeman's face. How stupid that would be. This policeman is Sipho-Smiler and not the one at the prison who turned Uncle and me away. I want violence, want to break something, smash a window, blow up the prison, blow up Soweto, blow up South Africa.

"Our education is important, Sergeant," Gloria says. "What can we say to the future if we do not fight for the things we want? What can we say to the future if we do not strive now for that which will later make us proud of ourselves?"

The dogs stop barking, pull off their collars, and stand up

straight. The policeman throws his police hat into the wings and becomes Sipho-Smiler again. We all group together facing Mosake's table, and, one by one, step forward addressing an imaginary person above Mosake's head.

Gloria speaks again.

"What can we say to the future?"

"Sorry, Future, I was drunk this week and all last week, so I couldn't be the doctor you wanted me to be. Oww, I'm very sorry, Future," one of the boys says, laughing loudly.

"Aii, Future. I'm sorry that you've got so few people who can read. I was too busy with my girlfriend to learn, but she's so nice and round, Future, and she kisses like a queen, Future. You can understand, hey?" somebody else says, stepping forward.

"Hey, Future, sorry that you have no black leaders, but we were too busy fighting among ourselves to think about you."

We all shake our heads and say together, "Sorry, Future."

"Future, I'm sorry there are no elephants or rhinos—I returned to the bush and shot them all because I needed to sell their horns. Hey, Future, I've got fifteen children and three wives who are hungry. You must understand, Future."

"Ya, Future, forgive him, Future, he's sorry he was so busy with his poaching he had no time to go to the family planning clinic," somebody else says, pointing at the last speaker.

"Future, Future, you must listen to me. I'm sorry, Future. I'm nowhere, Future. I didn't even know I had a future."

And Josh starts playing the piano and we sing a song about a lost future, and for a moment I think of Phakane. Did he think of his future when he joined the Action Committee? And did it include eight months in prison?

"Stop!" Mosake raps the table, interrupting our song. We break up and stand waiting for him to speak.

"Do any of you believe in what you're saying? You, Seraki, it sounded like you were reciting an advert for Lux soap. Don't you believe in what I've written?"

Everyone edges away from me. I feel the power of Mosake's focus.

"It's only a musical, not real life," I mumble.

"Is that what you think?"

"We are only playing here. These boys running around like dogs, it's stupid. This is only a game." I can't stop the anger that shoots out of me like bullets from a gun.

"You're wrong!" he shouts. "This is iSezela! It's only a game if you want it to be only that. The crocodile is out there and we must identify him in every way we can." Mosake picks up the crocodile on the table and holds it up high. He points to it. "We must expose him, show people what he is and how to overcome him." He squeezes the toy and the crocodile squeaks. Mosake tosses it back on the table and turns to us.

"This is not a musical, but a message." He walks among us, touching us, slapping a couple of the boys on their backs. "This is a message, not a musical. A message to the people. Do you understand?" Mosake stops in front of me, grips my shoulder, and shakes me. "Do you understand?"

I nod, trying to understand. It's like a light you can see, but then you can't. Can we really change people's minds with what we are doing? Is it possible that people will understand our message?

"And I want you to treat it as the most important message you have ever delivered. The crocodile is everywhere. You have all seen him, not so?" Mosake asks. One or two of the boys nod; the girls glance at one another. They agree. Only Nongeni looks puzzled. She might be too rich to understand what Mosake is talking about.

"Right! Let's take it from the top again. Dogs, you are not vicious enough. Sipho, what makes you think the police smile so easily? No smiling when you say your line. Cathy, we must get a hat that fits Sipho. This one makes him look ridiculous."

"Maybe that's a good idea," I say.

Mosake turns to me, thinks for a moment, and then laughs.

"Yes, excellent. Good, Seraki! Don't worry about the hat, Cathy, we'll keep it too big. Nongeni, can you at least look a little more frightened? Again, everyone. From the top."

Mosake is right. People need to hear this message. My house is surrounded by crocodiles and no amount of *muti* Mr. Nzule buys can keep them away. He needs to get this message, but will he be able to hear it?

We start over again, and I feel better about what I'm doing, but not about what happened this afternoon with Uncle. I don't like thinking about what went on at the prison. Something went very wrong today. A voice in the back of my mind tells me that maybe my uncle lied. I don't like hearing this.

From the alley I see two men standing in front of our house. Something is not right. I hear angry voices. I crouch in the shadows away from the kitchen light. The two men are lounging by the door, smoking cigarettes. They do not see me. They are Naughty Boys.

I creep along the wall of Mrs. Mcebi's house, and sprint around the yard to our back window. Crawling along the ground, I hear the voices clearly. Uncle is in there and he sounds afraid.

I make my way slowly to the back window. I see four strangers sitting around the table with my uncle. An ax lies between them. My uncle's back is shaking, his head is buried in his hands. I think he is crying.

"Hey, Vula, you're stupid, dumb, too, hey? Very stupid, not so?" one of them says.

He seems to be the leader. He's wearing a flashy white silk shirt, and has dark glasses on even though it's nighttime. The others are also gangsters. They wear scruffy clothes. One of them is wearing a soft hat, another a torn T-shirt. None is as smartly dressed as White Shirt.

My uncle nods.

"You come asking for information, we give it to you on condition you pay us, and then you try to sneak away. This man wants to live a short life," White Shirt says, picking up the ax from the table. "We know the police better than you do. We know how to get information out of them. There is no other way. You want to see your nephew, you pay us the money." He slams the ax into the table. With his big hands moving fast, he pulls at my uncle's hair, forces him down onto the table, pries loose the ax, and passes it to one of the other men.

I want to cry out, run away, not look, but I can't do anything. I watch.

White Shirt leans closer to Uncle's ear and whispers something. He is holding Uncle's neck, squashing his face into the table. Then he looks up and nods to the man with the ax. It crashes down in front of my uncle's face.

"We like you, Vula. You play a good saxophone, but don't try to cross us. We want the money you owe."

Voices come from the alley. Somebody shouts. It's Mr. Nzule. I dash to the edge of the house. The two Naughty Boys are pulling Mr. Nzule toward the door. I am back at the window. Mr. Nzule is on the floor. He is shouting, pleading.

"Very bad to have somebody like this in your house, Nzule. He could bring a lot of trouble to you," White Shirt says, and slaps Uncle. "I would be careful who you invite to stay."

The men are bending Mr. Nzule's arm. They drag him to the table, and push his face next to Uncle's. Mr. Nzule is pleading, squealing like a pig. He is afraid and I am afraid, but I don't know what to do. Nobody will come to help us if they know it's the Naughty Boys.

"Tough on kids like Phakane that they've got such useless family men," White Shirt says, and pulls Uncle's face off the table and slams it back down. The man holding Mr. Nzule does the same. My father screams. His nose is bleeding.

The men and the ax go out the door. I watch them walk down the alley and disappear.

Nobody is dead. Nobody is dying.

I run into the house and find Mr. Nzule glaring at Uncle.

"Uncle! What is going on?"

They look at me blankly. I don't think they see me. Mr. Nzule gets up, scoops water from a bowl, and splashes his face. His blood smears his cheeks and hands.

"They told me they could find out where Phakane's kept," Un-

52

cle moans. "They wanted money for the information, Nzule. But when Seraki and I went, Phakane was not there, so I didn't pay them the money. It's more than I have."

"How much?" I ask.

"Three hundred rand."

"I told you not to interfere!" Mr. Nzule swings around, shouting at my uncle. "Who asked you to bring those gangsters into my house? Who asked you to do anything?"

"Nzule, I was trying to help—"

"Get out! Get out!" Mr. Nzule screams. He throws the bowl at my uncle, who ducks and falls away from the table. I see his face for the first time. One of his eyes is puffed, half closed, and his lip is bleeding.

"You bring those people into my house, those people who will kill us like we kill flies. You deal with those people who burn houses, rob old women. You bring those people into my house! Get out! I never want you to cross my doorway again. Never!" Mr. Nzule moves toward Uncle. He has a knife in his hand.

"Nzule, wait, slow down. I meant no harm. I wish no danger to my sister's household . . ."

"Father, please don't . . ." Mr. Nzule does not hear me.

"If you come here again I will kill you. I swear it!"

"Nzule . . ." Uncle is stumbling backward to the door.

"Get out!"

Uncle is halfway down the alley, disappearing, and Mr. Nzule is behind him, screaming oaths. I am running too. I want to tell Uncle I have the money. I don't know when I will see him again.

"Uncle!" I shout after him. He stops. Mr. Nzule is behind me. He is calling me to come back inside. My uncle is at the corner. He is waving at me.

"I'm sorry, *mshana*. I will see you again, soon. I promise," he shouts.

"Wait! Uncle!"

"Seraki!" Mr. Nzule grabs my arm and pulls me back down the alley to the house. When I turn around my uncle is gone.

53

"You have chased my uncle away from our house. You cannot do that. He is always welcome," I shout at Mr. Nzule.

He strikes me hard across the head.

I fall.

Mr. Nzule grabs my arm and pulls me up.

"Get inside. I never want to hear you talk about that man again. Never! He will bring death to our house. He has destroyed the *muti* I paid so much for to protect our house."

Mr. Nzule pulls down the bags of powder and bones above the doorway and throws them over the fence. "These are useless now. It will cost much money to get more powerful *muti*."

"What about Phakane?"

"Your brother will come home when it's his time to come home. We can do nothing about that. I have tried—"

"Not hard enough!"

He hits me again. My head clangs as loud as his voice.

". . . talk to your parent like that. I am still your father. You will listen to me. Now go to bed!"

The door slams. My head pounds. I lie on the floor, in a pool of water with Mr. Nzule's blood. He is gone. Uncle is gone I don't know where. My mother is never here. Phakane is gone.

Three hundred rand for Phakane! Three hundred. Three hundred becomes the beat in my head. I lie on the floor until my thoughts start coming again and I decide that I won't go to school in the morning. I have to get word out on the streets. I cannot waste the time sitting at school, and I can't take time for sleeping either. I must begin right now by getting myself up from this floor. Mr. Nzule will be too drunk to see clearly when he comes home from Auntie Somoza's.

I stuff my pillow under the blanket on my bed and blow out the light of the lamp. I close the door behind me.

Somewhere I will find someone who knows White Shirt.

AUNTIE SOMOZA'S

Auntie Somoza always says it doesn't take a lot of beer to cause a lot of trouble. She should know. She says she's served enough beer in her time to drown fifty men, six dogs, and three cats. I don't know if this is true, but I don't argue with a shebeen queen who can crack a pair of *skollie* heads together like I would two walnuts. I've also heard the story about how Auntie took up a golf club and chased away five pimply white soldiers from the South African army, after they entered her shebeen looking for weapons without a warrant, and I know this story is true. I've seen the club.

Her shebeen is only one block away from the taxi stand, so when somebody has had enough to drink, she clicks her tongue against her teeth, waves her floppy, fat arms, and says, "There's only one block left in you, *wena*, time to go home." And then, ignoring all protests, she throws him out. She knows exactly how far her clients can stagger when they've seen too much of the bottom of their glasses. She also won't serve anyone she doesn't know, and for many, like Mr. Nzule, her place is a second home. I asked her once where *her* second home was and she laughed and said, "John Vorster Square, Seraki, the hell that all shebeen queens eventually get to." Anytime she's not at her shebeen you can bet she's been taken to police headquarters in Johannesburg again. And that's only one of the kinds of trouble you get serving beer.

I stand outside her shebeen and peer through the cracked window. It won't be hard to find Auntie Somoza, even among the big mid-week crowd. I just have to listen for her laugh. When she's in a good mood she can be heard down the street, across the sixth and seventh zones, and all over Soweto. She laughs as if laughing's the greatest and only thing worth doing in the world.

Inside, clients sit around tables cluttered with empty beer bottles. Others stand against the walls. The small room is full with people, smoke, reggae music, and—there it is—Auntie Somoza's laugh. Then I hear glass breaking. For an instant everything is still and I catch a glimpse of Auntie Somoza.

She is at one of the tables, standing over a man staring down at a broken glass. He looks up. It's Mr. Nzule. I duck. If he catches me, he'll make my head clang for a week. I can't let him see me, but I have to talk to Auntie Somoza. I'll wait for her around the back. Sooner or later she will come outside to fetch more beer.

Voices follow me down the path, and I slide into the shadow of the storeroom, into the stink of sick and urine.

"I tell you! She does!" says one voice.

Two men walk up the side of the storeroom and turn their faces to the wall.

"But she wouldn't have any business left . . . ," his friend argues.

They're very drunk and their words come out more slowly than their piss.

"I tell you I can taste the water! It's there, in everything she serves," the first man says.

"If there's so much water in her booze, how come you can't walk straight?" His friend laughs, falling over a bottle lying in his way. The first man has no answer to that.

"You letting all my good booze run to waste?" Auntie Somoza says, blocking the back door of the shebeen with her great rhino body. The two men have to squeeze past her to get back to their beer as she pulls a bunch of keys from the front of her dress. Her giant shadow moves toward me and she unlocks the storeroom door.

"Auntie! Psst! Auntie!" I whisper.

"Yi!" she yelps, and spins around, closing her hand on my shoulder like a clamp.

I wriggle and try to free myself. "Hey, wait! It's me! Seraki!"

"What are you doing here, boy?"

"I want to ask you something, something to do with Phakane."

Her grip slackens. "Your father's inside, and he is not in a good mood."

"I know, but Auntie, there's been big trouble." The thought of Mr. Nzule coming out and finding us makes me talk fast. "Some men were at our house just now. I'm sure they were Naughty Boys. One was wearing a shiny white silk shirt and had dark glasses on. He said that for three hundred rand they can find Phakane." I'm too ashamed to tell her what happened between Mr. Nzule and Uncle, so I ask her straight out. "Can you tell me who he is?"

Auntie Somoza swears, spits, and lets go of my shoulder.

"So King Danny's on the loose again, is he? Just let him come asking for booze around here! I'll spike his drinks with paraffin!"

"You know him?"

"Yes, but I don't want you to. The Naughty Boys are bad people, Seraki. Very bad." Auntie spits again. "Especially that King Danny. Instead of doing honest work they *skelem* money out of people who can't afford their next meal. They buy the police, buy women, schoolgirls, too, anything they want they have. They know everything in the township—who's bought a new car, who's daughter is ripe for lovemaking, who's got a salary increase, everything."

"Auntie, I have to talk to them. The Naughty Boys are the only ones . . . Even Uncle . . . Since the police took Phakane away we've heard nothing about him."

"King Danny comes here sometimes, but not often. My place isn't good enough for him." She snorts. "And I don't know where he lives."

"Auntie, can I wait for him here until he comes again?"

"But your father . . ."

"He doesn't have to know. Please!"

She thinks for a minute, then asks, "And what can you do about Phakane, hey?"

"I can get most of the money."

"How?"

"I can get it, and not by stealing either. Just say I can wait here for King Danny. Please, Auntie!"

She looks hard at me and then turns back toward the noise coming through the open door. Finally she grins, cuffs the side of my head, and goes back inside.

She didn't say I couldn't. She didn't say anything. So I can. I can wait here for King Danny—every night if I have to. I will wait here to do my business with White Shirt and the Naughty Boys.

I hate this scene we're rehearsing today. It reminds me too much of Sweets. She's a girl in our zone I know who used to have a smile as wide as her breasts.

We sit in a classroom, and Teddy, the comic of the cast, is playing a blubbering, drunken school principal, just like it really is. He stumbles around the classroom, mumbling his lessons, and taking a drink from the bottle hidden in his jacket.

We sit at our desks, bored, frustrated, just like it really is.

The gangsters rush into our classroom. They hold knives and axes. They're looking for a schoolgirl.

Nobody moves, everyone is frightened, just like it really is.

We huddle to one side of the room while they pull Gloria out from her desk.

The principal pretends he doesn't see them. He writes another algebra sum on the blackboard.

Gloria is dragged out of the classroom.

We do not see them rape her, but we hear her screams.

My skin goes prickly. It's too real. It's just like it really is.

This happens in the township a lot. We call it jackrolling. The gangs come looking for schoolgirls and nobody stops them. Not the principals, not the police, not anybody. Nobody dares. Mosake is taking a chance showing this scene. People will agree with it in their hearts, but nobody will say anything out loud.

We come together around the empty desk where Gloria used to sit, and sing the jackrolling song:

58

How can we learn
   when we are not safe?
How can we grow
   when we are threatened?
Who will protect us
   from the terror of these men?
What chance do we have,
   if we do not stop this evil?
iSezela, we are watching you,
iSezela, your time is over!

Once I planned for Sweets to be my girlfriend, but not anymore. She's different since the Naughty Boys have had her. Now she is nothing but another spoiled beauty who's been jackrolled. I still see Sweets every now and then, and watch how people talk to her without looking at her. Some feel sorry for her, but a lot of people blame her for wearing her school dresses so short, for making herself look like a challenge for the Naughty Boys. I don't know what I think. I'm somewhere in between, but every time we sing this song I think of Sweets.

iSezela, we are watching you
Burn iSezela, to be free!

Some of the girls cry when we sing this song. I mean real tears. Sometimes I feel the same, but I hold back my tears. I cannot cry for Sweets and I will not cry for Phakane. He would not want me to.

Instead, I will find King Danny and I will see my brother. Uncle has failed. Adults can't always be trusted to make things right. This is something I must do by myself. If I were the one in prison, I know Phakane would feel the same way. He would wait for King Danny. Maybe tonight will be my last night of waiting.

The song ends. Silence. Mosake holds us with his eyes. Cathy and Josh are still. Even Oswald has stopped chewing on his pencil. The air in the rehearsal room won't let the song go. If you listen carefully you can still hear our voices. We have never sung it so well. Mosake is pleased.

"Good! That's the kind of intensity I like to see," he calls from his table. "Now, a couple of you boys, grab that sheet over there and string it up across the hall here. Once you've had your costumes fitted and checked, we'll call it a day. And when they are ready, you must look after them yourselves. If they get dirty or torn, you must get them fixed. You don't get onto my stage unless your costume is right and—"

Oswald, fat as ever, interrupts Mosake.

"These costumes cost me a lot of money," he says, again chewing on his pencil. "Anyone ruins them and he'll have money taken off his wages." He stabs his stubby finger right at me.

Mosake looks sharply at Fat-man Oswald, and says to us, "Don't forget, everybody! Tomorrow's Saturday and we move our rehearsal onto the stage. You all know where it is?"

We nod. We know where the auditorium is. We've been looking forward to this for weeks.

Then, for no reason I can see, Mosake is suddenly angry. He pulls Oswald to one side of the room. Mosake points to us, and Oswald bangs his fist into his palm. I can't make out what they are saying but they are arguing. Cathy looks up and frowns. Then she leaves the girl she is tucking and pinning, and walks over to them. They both look at her startled and quickly leave the room.

Cathy comes back to us.

"I think everyone's a little weary today. Come on, let's get this fitting finished so we can all go home," she says.

I'm tired too. I've been waiting up every night behind Auntie Somoza's for almost two weeks, and all this singing and dancing, and now the squealing of the girls behind the sheet, is giving me a headache.

It's only a costume fitting and they are acting like it's the greatest event yet. How stupid. We'll only be wearing school uniforms, traditional tribal costumes, and brightly colored T-shirts and pants. Everything of mine fits fine and I'm bored watching Josh check the boys' costumes. He says we can't go out from behind this curtain till the girls are finished.

"Could you all just quieten down, please!" calls Cathy from the girls' side of the sheet. "And do yourselves up quickly. Josh, when you're finished with the boys, have them line up so I can check them too."

We shuffle over to where Cathy is pointing and line up. She and Josh are going to check us again, one by one.

This will take forever. Josh is just looking, but Cathy is making little notes and pinning them onto each costume.

"That's fine," she says. "Now, Gloria, I need you to put on the red silk dress and then come back here. I want to straighten the hemline."

Gloria looks fantastic as she swishes by. Some of the boys edge along the sheet, trying to peer around its corner to watch Gloria change. Cathy's too quick for them, and she moves us all back so we can't see. Stupid. I'll bet every boy here's seen more than what Gloria's got to show.

I lean against the wall, waiting for Josh to get to me. I hate this waiting around.

"It feels funny to be wearing school uniforms in a musical," Nongeni says, standing beside me. Maybe she doesn't think I'm a gangster like the rest of them probably do.

"I'd like to burn mine," I say, and then wish I hadn't. It was a stupid thing to say.

"I'm Nongeni."

"I know."

Silence. She looks around, like she's feeling as nervous talking to me as I am talking to her. I don't know what to say next.

"Mosake is becoming more tense, don't you think?" she says. "He always gets like this before opening night."

"What's he got to worry about? We're the ones on the stage," I say, and realize I must sound irritated. I'm tired and can't concentrate. I want to go home. No, I don't want to go home. Mr. Nzule will be there, and Uncle will not.

"Is this your first time on stage?"

"Yes."

"You're very good—I mean you sing very well."

Pause. We are both struggling to get our dripping words off the clothesline.

"It's so exciting, don't you think?"

"I suppose."

"It's all I've ever really wanted to do," she says. "I've always wanted to be in a Mosake musical."

Gloria is back out from behind the sheet, and I can't keep my eyes off her. It's the way she walks, the easy movement of her hips, her tight-fitting costume. She knows she looks like a movie star. She glides past the boys to where Cathy is standing and hops onto the chair for Cathy to check her hem. Nongeni notices me looking.

"You like Gloria?"

"She's okay."

"I think all the boys like her."

"Uh-huh."

"Well, I'll see you tomorrow. Cathy wants me next," she says, and moves away.

I didn't mean to be rude to her, but I'm not used to talking to high-class girls. And I'm too tired to be polite so I wait by myself for my costume to be checked.

Finally the stupid rehearsal is over, and I leave the hall, glad to be outside in the dust and noise of real life, and on my way home.

How can Nongeni take the musical so seriously? Hasn't she anything else to think about but Mosake and his show?

I have to get home quickly. It's Friday night; money and booze are in the air. Maybe tonight King Danny will come. He has to come soon. I won't be able to wait past next Friday. Our opening is Saturday. I have to talk with White Shirt before Saturday night.

I have to tell him that it won't be long until I have the full three hundred. And if the show does run for an extra week, like Mosake says it might—he says the bookings are doing well—then I'll have money left over. Ten rand a performance! I'll have ninety rand extra, but I won't tell King Danny that.

Only twelve more blocks till I'm home. I jump over the fence and run through the municipal park. The tall industrial lamps are shining down on the township like yellow moons. The night is a dull, sick yellow color. Soon the air will be thick with insects swarming around each light. The dogs will come out, too, and run in packs at the people who aren't home safely, or not so safely inside the shebeens.

I wonder if Cathy is Mosake's woman? She looks at him in that way sometimes. Like Gloria smiled at me, again, today. I don't care if all the boys are after her. I want her. She smiled at me like she knew what I was thinking.

OPENINGS

I am sitting in the shadows where I can watch both the front and back of Auntie Somoza's shebeen. After all these nights this spot is almost comfortable and I am having trouble keeping my eyes open. It must be well past midnight. Already there's a big crowd inside, and more people are walking up the path to the front door. A couple of times, after I dozed off, I had to get up to peek through the window. There's still no King Danny. I must be patient. Auntie Somoza is sure he'll come tonight.

I'm beginning to recognize Auntie's clients. That man there, he's the pastor! All kinds come to her shebeen—policemen, taxi drivers, schoolteachers, even some housewives. It seems that Auntie's is good enough for most people, but maybe not for King Danny.

Thinking about the money helps me stay awake. I've already made one hundred and nineteen rand—more money than I've ever had in my life. I can feel the pouch hanging from my neck inside my shirt. It is heavy. I like feeling the weight of it and looking inside and seeing all my money. I like having money. People with money can do things.

Mr. Nzule comes out the front door of Auntie Somoza's. I crouch

63

deeper into the shadows and watch as he fumbles with the latch of the gate. He stumbles down the street, swearing and kicking at the dogs lying in his path. He never knows when he's had too much to drink and when it's time for him to go. Often Auntie Somoza throws him out with the last of her clients. Sometimes I wonder how he gets home. I hate seeing him stagger out of the shebeen every night. One night I watched him fall, and couldn't move to help him.

That night, maybe it was last Tuesday, Auntie Somoza told me how sometimes things get too heavy for people, that they can't take the weight, and they collapse. She said my father's carrying too much weight right now, that he's worried about Phakane, and about me. I can't believe that. When did he ever worry about me?

I want to tell Mr. Nzule about the musical. I want him to come to opening night next week and be proud of me. I've tried to tell him, but there never seems to be the right moment.

When I told my mother about the musical a few weeks ago she was pleased. She doesn't smile often, but I got her laughing when I sang a chorus for her. I could tell she was proud of me. She promised to ask her madam for the night off so she could see our opening. The madam won't come. She doesn't care about the people who work for her. Ma is supposed to be home every night, but she isn't. Her madam often keeps her late until she misses the last bus to the township and we never know when she will be home.

Now, even when she's home, the mood in our house is sticky, and I hate being home. Ever since Uncle left, Ma won't talk to Mr. Nzule, or to me. She doesn't want to hear about what really happened. She's blaming me for something I don't understand, and she's angry with Mr. Nzule for chasing Uncle away. Nobody says anything, and I'm afraid to mention Uncle, or the show. I am angry with Mr. Nzule. And hurt and angry with my uncle for running away. Uncle knows how things work. He understands the way things should be and has such good ideas. But why is it his thoughts never turn into anything real?

A white car pulls up in front of the shebeen. The lights blind me and I crouch farther back into the shadows. Four men get out and walk up the path. King Danny is one of them. He's wearing the same kind of silk shirt that he wore that night at our house. The other three hang back so King Danny is the first to go through the door.

"Seraki! Pssst, Seraki!" Auntie Somoza hisses into the darkness.

"I know! I know! I saw him, but how am I going to get him outside?"

"Don't worry, nature will take care of that!" She chuckles and goes back inside.

It's a long time before King Danny opens the door and comes into the backyard. He stands against the wall and unzips his fly. I wait until he's nearly done, and then stand up.

"King Danny?"

There's a flash of a knife, and he's got me by the throat.

"Who you, boy?" he growls.

I can hardly breathe, let alone answer. He slams me against the wall and looks at me.

"Stupid boy! Creeping up on people like that!" He lets go of my throat and moves toward the house.

"Wait! Please don't go. It's about Phakane! My brother, Phakane. You know? You spoke to my uncle about getting him out of prison. I have the money!"

He stops at the door and turns.

"You got money?"

"Yes." I pull my pouch over my head and hand it to him. "I know you want three hundred, but I can only give you what I have now. I have a job."

He holds the pouch in the light and pulls out the wad of notes. I've never seen anyone count money so fast. Then he has it all in his pocket.

"There's only a hundred and nineteen rand here."

"I'm getting more. In a month's time I'll have the rest."

"You want to see your brother?"

"Yes. And I want him to come home. You said you could get him out."

"I know where he is, but as for getting him out . . ." He doesn't finish.

"But you said that three hundred would . . ."

"The price's gone up. It's more difficult now, and of course there's the interest on your uncle's bad debt." He turns to go, stops, and turns back to look at me.

"How long have you been waiting for me?"

"Tonight and many other nights. Over two weeks."

"Every night?"

"Yes."

He comes toward me, pulls me into the light, and looks closely at me. "Meet me at Ikwezi Station tomorrow afternoon. Three o'clock," he says.

"Three o'clock. Tomorrow. Ikwezi," I repeat after him, and then quickly add, "Don't tell my father."

"You've got more guts than your father, boy, but there's one thing you better learn: Never creep up on a man like that. You could get yourself killed."

I watch the back of his silk shirt disappear into the shebeen. I've done it! Tomorrow I'm going to see Phakane! I want to run inside and tell Auntie Somoza, but I stop myself. I remember the last time I felt like this and nothing happened. That doesn't matter now. Tomorrow will be different. I will be going with King Danny. I will see Phakane.

I am not tired anymore. Tomorrow, come quickly. Three o'clock Saturday. Three o'clock?

My heart jolts and I stop running toward home. Tomorrow, three o'clock, we'll be rehearsing on the stage for the first time. I've never been on a stage before . . . and I won't be there. But I must see Phakane! This is my only chance.

Mosake will understand. With all his talk about fighting the crocodiles, and beating them, he is sure to accept my not being there. Mosake will understand.

When I get home my mother is not there. The house is in a mess and full of the smell of sick. Mr. Nzule is snoring loudly on the

66

floor. Next to him, the primus stove is hissing and water is bubbling over. He must have fallen asleep before he could get mealies into the pot. I turn off the small stove. I want to get him into bed. He can't hear me and he's too heavy to lift.

I take a pillow, push it under his head, and cover him with blankets. I wish I could talk to him.

I wish he was someone else, someone stronger.

King Danny is standing in the doorway of the prison.

"Go, you've got twenty minutes."

I stare at him.

"Go, quickly, or they may change their minds."

I walk into the prison. Gray walls, steel bars, big men who walk loudly in polished brown boots down echoing corridors. Behind a thick glass window a policeman sits at an office desk covered with papers. He's using a cracked coffee cup as an ashtray, and there's a photograph of his family. On the wall behind him, shotguns in a rack point to the ceiling, and pictures of strange-looking men stare down from a brown board.

I hear the policeman's cigarette go *phit* as he tosses it into the cup. He gets up from the desk and leads me down the corridor and into a small, dirty room. He tells me to wait. I sit on the edge of the wobbly chair.

I wait.

I know this time it must be the right prison. My brother is somewhere inside. The policeman standing guard at the door keeps looking at me. I stare back at him. I don't want to look as frightened as I feel. He closes the door.

My insides are jiggling around and I can't sit still. I can't stop thinking about what it will be like to see Phakane, to touch him, to hear my brother talk. I walk back and forth, counting the blocks on the floor.

On our way here one of my friends saw me get on the train with King Danny. He looked surprised. I could tell he wanted to know what I was doing with a Naughty Boy. He'll probably tell everyone that he saw me. What do I care? It doesn't matter. I'll be the one who saw Phakane. Even if someone is stupid enough to tell Mr. Nzule I was with the Naughty Boys, he won't beat me after I tell him I've seen Phakane.

I wait longer.

Maybe they have changed their minds. Maybe King Danny has tricked me. Maybe it's the wrong prison. Maybe they won't let me out. Maybe Phakane is not here at all.

Everything is quiet and I am still, except for my insides, which run about, up and down my stomach, up through my throat, into my head, whiz around my brain, and then rush down to my stomach again. I try to sit still, try to stop the tapping of my foot against the cement. There is a scraping noise, a rattling of keys, an iron door opening, slamming. A small box in the door slides open and I see one eye, half a nose, half a mouth.

I stare at the half-face.

It disappears.

The door opens and Phakane walks in.

We look at each other. I let out a long breath at the sight of him. My brother is the same as I remember, not any different.

We are hugging. He is laughing, saying "Seraki" over and over. I am hugging him, slapping his back. We are jumping up and down. Half-face is watching us.

"Seraki! Little brother how did you—"

"Hey brother, brother, I came here with—"

Our words tumble out on top of each other.

"How did you find me, Seraki?"

"The Naughty Boys," I whisper, and smell the prison on him. He does not smell like my brother.

"You know them?"

"I gave them money and they brought me here. I wanted to see you. I had to see you."

"What's happening outside? Our father, how is he? And Mom, what is she doing? And school? What are you doing with yourself?"

"How are you? What's it like inside? Do you eat enough? When are you coming home?" We laugh as our questions clash.

68

"You answer first, Seraki."

We are talking louder now and sitting on the chairs. I look closely at him. Mother's soft brown eyes still shine from his face; his hair is shaved off, which makes him look thinner; and his cheeks are a little hollow, making him look older.

"They are well, missing you. School's boring, and I'm in a musical and Uncle was here and . . ." I decided before not to mention Uncle, but now I've told Phakane and there's no getting out of it.

"Uncle! Is he here?"

"No, he has left, but he said he will be back. He had a fight with Mr. Nzule and left suddenly."

"That sounds like Uncle Vula and Dad!"

I know this disappoints my brother. He pulls his chair closer. Now our knees are touching. Phakane is leaning forward, holding both my hands, and we look hard at each other like we have never seen each other before. We are laughing. Nobody has said anything funny.

"Now you, Phakane . . ."

"I'm fine, fine. You mustn't worry. We have things worked out in here. And the food's not bad, but there's too much potatoes. I miss sugar. We only get one dollop of syrup with our tea."

Phakane looks quickly at the box in the door. Half-face is still watching.

"What do you think of these blue clothes, Seraki? A-one prison clothes they are. My very own costume," he says loudly, and then in a whisper, "I don't know when I'm coming out. You're not allowed to see me. No one is allowed. I'm classified an A-group prisoner. But obviously somebody was bribed to let you come in."

Now he is talking about the prison, the food, a square of blue sky, the hard floor, the other men, the prison wardens, and the scorpions that visit him at night. His voice is deeper and filled with the same power that sometimes Uncle's voice has.

I nod and watch him, trying to understand, trying not to stare at my brother and the fire in his eyes.

"How did you get the money?"

69

His question jolts me.

"I am in a musical. I am getting paid to sing and dance."

Phakane laughs. "You can't expect me to believe that!"

"Mr. Mosake is putting on a show in the township and I am in it. It's about Soweto and our lives . . . and a crocodile." I stumble. I can't explain. I know I understood what our musical was about when Mosake told us, and yet now I don't know what it's about and Phakane is looking at me, puzzled.

"I get money from rehearsing. We are having our opening night in two and a half weeks, and then I will be getting more money for the performances. I think you would like it."

"What does Dad say about it?"

"He doesn't know . . ."

We hear the box in the door slide shut and I watch as my brother changes in front of me. His face hardens, his mouth tightens, and an angry gleam comes into his eyes. He frowns and there are lines on his forehead that I have never noticed before. He looks serious. He looks like an adult.

"We won't have long now, Seraki. He's going to come back for us in two minutes, so listen carefully. I'm considering joining the hunger strike. Other prisoners have already begun. We've decided that the police can no longer hold us without charges or a fair trial. State of Emergency or not. It is time we did something about our position ourselves. Soon the whole country will hear about the hunger strikers in the prisons, and we're hoping that the government will do something about us."

"You're not going to eat anymore?"

"Once I have started I will not stop my fast until I have signed my release documents. It's an undertaking I'm prepared to die for. I have prepared myself psychologically. Either I am released or I will die."

Why is he talking about not eating, about death? I am puzzled by the sparkle that dances in the blackness of his eyes. This is something new in Phakane, and it is much stronger than anything I remember. It frightens me.

"But Phakane there must be some other way . . ."

70

"Seraki, you've got to understand: This is my only weapon as a prisoner to set myself free."

The box in the door slides open. Half-face is back. He looks at us, then disappears.

The door opens.

Phakane gets up. "It's time to go. Don't say anything about what I've told you. We have to organize things first. You will hear about us," he whispers.

"I will try and come back. Maybe bring Dad . . ."

"They are moving me tomorrow. I don't know where to. I will be home soon. I promise you. We are strong inside here. Sometimes I think stronger than when we are outside."

We are hugging. Phakane feels stiff, thin, wiry. He is taller than I remember. I want to hug all of him into my body until he is completely inside me, so that when I walk through the prison gates he is safely hidden away.

"Take my love home, Seraki. Take it to our parents."

"I will see you again."

"Be careful, brother."

The door closes. Phakane is gone.

And before I realize it I am outside in the sunshine.

I walk away from the gray building. I look up and down the street for King Danny. He is nowhere. I turn and look back at the prison, at the broken bottles cemented to the top of the high walls, the barbed wire, the watchtowers at four points of the prison.

Inside, Phakane is back in his cell, on his hard floor, with his square of blue sky and the scorpions. Outside, people are walking down the street, buying groceries, climbing into taxis, and going home. Here everything looks normal. I feel guilty to be running to catch a train, when I know Phakane can't. How can a hunger strike be a weapon? It will only kill him. I can't see him anymore in my mind, but I hear his words: Either I am released or I will die. What has happened to Phakane? I have never seen him so serious, so committed before. But I can't think about it now.

I am later than late.

It will be six o'clock before I get to the new place with the stage.

71

The train is going too slowly.

The rehearsal will be almost over. I have no time now to think of Phakane, but I know something has changed in my brother. And it frightens me. I will have to think about our visit later, when I have time to remember it all carefully.

ON CUE

Bastard!

I've never missed a rehearsal before. I've always been on time. I've always done everything he wanted me to do. I'll never go back! Never! There are other ways to get the money.

I run faster, ignoring the knife point of pain in my side. As my feet pound the pavement, all I can think of is wanting to get away, wanting to take off into the sky, sweep over the setting sun, and come crashing down into the earth somewhere else.

I don't care who he is, the bastard! Nobody treats me like that! I hate him!

My neck still aches where he grabbed me. I can still see the squeaking, squealing crocodile he shoved into my face. I tried to back away. I couldn't. Mosake held my head, held the crocodile so close to my face that I could see the red gleam in its eye, see its teeth, and see into its gaping mouth. I remembered the last time I touched the crocodile—red drops oozing from the palm of my hand.

He wouldn't let me say anything. Why didn't he let me explain? He's thrown me out.

To hell with Mister Big-time Mosake and his musical. I don't care about his stupid songs and dances, or his message. All I care about is getting the money. He's cut me off from the money I still owe to King Danny, and if I don't pay, King Danny will come around to the house again, and my father will find out, and there will be more trouble . . .

An ax crashing down onto the table. This time it will not be Uncle's face, but the faces of my mother and Mr. Nzule that are held inches from the blade. I have to get the money to pay King Danny! He won't care where it comes from. There's plenty of ways to get that kind of money. A couple of car jobs, maybe break into a house, do a bag snatch on a Friday-night train.

I reach the municipal park, jump over the fence. Only twelve more blocks to go.

"Seraki!"

Someone's calling me. I catch my breath and look around.

"Over here."

A girl is sitting on one of the swings. She stands up and waves.

"It's me! Nongeni!"

What's she doing here? What can I say to her? She saw what happened. I'll just wave her off and go on running. I'll pass her quickly and be out of this park . . .

"Wait! Don't go!"

No good! She's running up to me.

"What are you doing here?" she asks, panting.

"I'm on my way home. I always come this way. How did you get here so quickly?"

"I always come here after rehearsal and unwind. My dad picks me up and then drops me off here."

I'm sweating and I look past her to the traffic on the street outside the park. I should be running in that traffic, not standing here talking to her. I've got nothing to say and it feels strange to be seeing her away from the others. She's as surprised at seeing me here as I am at seeing her.

"I live down the road. This is a place I come to when I have to get away—from my parents mostly. They can be so stuffy sometimes that I need a place to breathe. This park is okay. You live round here?"

"No, on the other side. We don't have a proper house," I say, knowing what she's thinking.

"Oh."

I was abrupt with her again, so I search around in my head to find something else to say, but she's already talking.

"I'm sorry about what happened this afternoon."

I can tell from her face that she means it.

I wish I could tell her why I was late. I want to talk about Phakane—how great it was to see him, how gray the prison was, how frustrating it was speaking to him for only twenty minutes, how he spoke about dying and how it frightened me—but I can't. It's something I can't talk about yet to anyone. So I lie.

"I made a mistake. I thought the rehearsal was at the old place." I can see in her eyes that she doesn't believe me.

"I don't think Mosake meant what he said this afternoon. We need you in the musical. You're one of the best. Please don't stop coming. I'm sure he—"

"I won't go anywhere near him! You heard what he said." I don't need her to remind me of how I walked into the hall when everyone was on the stage, how Sipho pointed at me and the rehearsal stopped, how Mosake made a fool of me, how he shouted at me in front of the whole cast, stuffed the crocodile into my face, screaming worse than Mr. Nzule does when he's drunk.

"He was in a bad mood even before you came," she is saying. "It wasn't all your fault. The run-through was terrible. It always is the first time on the stage. Everything goes wrong. It's natural, until everyone gets used to the new space. The bad rehearsal had nothing to do with you—and Mosake knows it. He was only using you to get angry at the rest of us. You should have seen him during the rehearsal. He shouted at Sipho and Tisha, and almost had Gloria crying."

I wait for her to go on.

"You still want to be in the musical, don't you?"

Suddenly the thought of not being in the musical hits me. It's the main thing I do nowadays. I can't remember what I did with my time before all this started. I will miss singing with the others, and dancing with Gloria. And it's more than just missing it. It hurts me inside to think about not doing it anymore. After all this time, how can I not be there on opening night?

"Yes, I do," I reply.

"Then come on Monday," she says, smiling, and I think she is planning something.

"What can—"

"I'll phone Cathy and speak to her. If I need to I'll talk to Mosake. I'm sure he didn't mean what he said today and by Monday he will have calmed down. We need you, and Josh nearly freaked when Mosake said you were out of the show."

I like hearing this. I'd like to hear more, so I ask, "Do you really think you can fix it up?"

"Yes, but you'll have to be there early."

"Okay, I'll be there," I say, feeling that maybe things aren't so bad. "Come, Nongeni, and I'll push you on the swing."

Her feet are flying over my head and we are laughing and she is yelling for me to stop, stop. And I will stop but first I have to think about what she will do. She says that Mosake needs me. That he will take me back. He must take me back. I will not be beaten. Once I'm back in the musical I'll have the money and I won't have to think about doing a bag snatch or a car job.

We sit on the swings, moving slowly back and forth together. Nongeni knows all about musicals, and she is even more excited than I am about being in this one. She says working with Mosake is a dream come true, and I want to laugh at that, but I don't, not out loud anyway. Until today, being in this musical didn't seem like work at all to me, and all my dreams are of Phakane coming home.

Nongeni knows a lot about "the business," as she calls it, and in a funny way I'm finding it interesting. I didn't know for sure that Cathy is Mosake's latest lover, or that there's serious trouble between Mosake and Fat Oswald. They had another big fight today, she says, and I'm glad to hear it. Maybe she's also right that Mosake wasn't only angry at me.

I didn't have any idea how jealous Nongeni is of Gloria for

getting to sing all the solo numbers. She makes me promise not to tell.

It's dark when I say good-bye to Nongeni.

I run out of the park thinking what a strange day I've had. I was thrown out of the musical, I met Nongeni in a park and became friends with her, and the strangest part of all was my trip with King Danny to see Phakane.

Uncle was wrong: Phakane was different, even though he was the same. He wasn't like a saxophone left out in the yard. He was like a brother who goes away to another country and comes back talking funny and using new words. He looks the same, but his voice was stronger than before.

How will a hunger strike change anything? I can't work this out and I wish Uncle was around to tell me. If you go on a hunger strike, when do you know if it's finished? When do you know to eat again? How can hungry prisoners make anything happen? I think starving yourself to death is stupid, until I remember the sparkle in Phakane's eyes. That sparkle was determination. It had something to do with a spirit stronger than anything I have ever seen in my brother before.

I run through the circle of light where some Naughty Boys are throwing dice on the pavement. Their secret words float in the air behind me.

"Tricky sixes, come to Rich Boy!"

"Hip-hop four, go out the door!"

I don't run around them or stop to watch. They are small, shrunken, like children playing games, compared to Phakane and those other men in prison.

I walk slowly down the alley toward my house. I want to tell my parents I have seen Phakane, but I don't know if I should. After what Phakane said about the hunger strike I don't think I can. And they'll want to know how I managed it, and then I'll have to tell them about giving all that money to King Danny.

Just because I've seen him doesn't mean he's coming home, and they may get excited and then be disappointed. Phakane said that we would hear about him. I'll have to wait for that. Besides, Mr.

Nzule will be furious about King Danny, and about the money and my going without him. He'll say I should have told him first.

But I want to tell them Phakane's all right, that he's healthy and strong, that he sends his love to them and wishes he could be home. I want to tell my mother how he looks, how we jumped together, and how he squeezed me. And how brave he is. I must tell her how brave he is. She needs to hear that.

I stop a little way before our house. Inside there is a light on. Someone's inside. I watch and wait. I have to make sure it isn't King Danny. I can't hear anything. And then the shadow of my mother passes the window, and I know everything is normal. Only it's so quiet I wonder if Mr. Nzule is at home. But now he's coming through the door and bending down to pick up a brick.

From the shadow of Mrs. Mcebi's house, I watch as he bangs something into our door frame. I want to call to him but I don't. Even if I don't like coming home anymore, Phakane would give anything to walk up this alley and stand where I'm standing now, watching him nail fresh *muti* to our door.

It is quiet and my parents are at home. I will tell them I've seen Phakane. I have to tell them, even if it makes Mr. Nzule angry.

Mr. Nzule turns around. He freezes, the brick in his left hand, staring at me as if he has never seen me before. He has a strange look on his face.

"Phakane?" he calls out, and I step out of the shadows. "Oh Seraki, it's you. Come inside, your mother has made supper." He pats me on the back, and pushes me gently inside.

He looks tired, and I'm surprised that he seems pleased to see me.

I greet my mother, sit down at the table, and wait for her to serve the food. It is warm inside, but I shiver, imagining Phakane standing in the corner of the room watching over us. He would love to be here eating with us at this table.

"You called me Phakane just now. Do I look a lot like him?" I ask.

My mother stops serving. They glance at each other.

"No, I just thought . . ." He stops, and my mother turns quickly back to the food. "I just thought for a moment it was Phakane standing there. That's all."

"Here, Seraki, eat." Ma comes back to the table and places the food in front of me. She turns to Mr. Nzule and puts his plate in front of him with more force. "And you, Nzule, stop dreaming so much. Soon you will see our son's ghost walking in this room. And it will be here because you are wishing for him so much that his spirit will leave his body to be here. And then after you have seen him, the spirit won't find its way back to our son's body. And we will have lost Phakane twice."

Mr. Nzule eats silently, avoiding the pain in my mother's eyes. Doesn't he notice how she is hurting?

She has never scolded him like this before. I should not have mentioned my brother's name. I made Mr. Nzule talk of him in front of her. She doesn't like hearing talk of him.

Even if I tell them about my visit today, it will not make Phakane come home. He may be away for a long time still. My mother will not be happy until Phakane is actually here. I remember when Uncle took me to the prison and I didn't see my brother. If I tell them about today, they will be as disappointed as I was that day. And what can I say to them about King Danny?

No, I cannot tell them about seeing Phakane.

We're backstage waiting for Mosake to arrive. It's funny to think all this tension is because of me. Everyone is looking at me, but I stand off by myself. Cathy comes up onto the stage and calls us all together. I look at Nongeni. She said she had talked to Cathy on the phone Saturday night.

"Now listen, everyone," Cathy says. "When Mosake comes, you must start at once. I've told Josh to go straight into the opening number. Get into your positions now."

She comes over to me and whispers, "Seraki, you had better put everything you have into this rehearsal. It's the only thing that may change his mind."

The auditorium door opens. Mosake comes in and sits down at the back.

As we quickly prepare for the opening number, Sipho-Smiler grips my hand. "I hope you're coming back," he says.

"Thanks."

Josh strikes the opening chord and I run onto the stage, punch the air with my fist, and let out the loudest, truest sound I can find in my chest. I know Mosake is watching me from somewhere out there in the dim light of the auditorium. All I want to think about is doing what I have done so often before, only better.

There's no reaction from the back of the theater.

We work our way through the musical. I feel the others supporting me, pushing me forward, giving me center stage, and I perform, pull everything out and send it all to that shape that's Mosake at the back of the theater. And then, before we know it, the first half of the show is finished.

Josh stops playing and looks across the rows of seats to Mosake. Cathy's there, leaning toward him, saying something. We stand silently on stage, looking into the dark of the auditorium.

We wait.

"Carry on," she calls.

We start the second half and our story moves toward its climax. We've never done it so well. For the first time it feels like we are connected to one another, working together, with one mind.

We're only moments before the end when Sipho-Smiler fumbles his line. He's jumped ahead in the script and now even Gloria is thrown off her cue. She turns to me with something I've never heard before. I forget my place and mumble my next line, which doesn't make sense now. I hesitate, try to pick up the dialogue with another line that I know is wrong, and then I stop. I look around. Nongeni, waiting for her cue in the wings, has her hands clamped over her mouth. Everyone is dazed.

Josh lifts his eyes from his score and whispers something I can't hear. What's happened to us? Why couldn't we make it to the end? We were almost there, and now nobody knows where we are, or what comes next. Our perfect run-through has come to a dead stop.

"Okay, okay! Enough!"

Mosake gets up from his seat and walks down the aisle.

We know what's coming: He's furious.

"Good. That was much better. Much better!" Mosake says, jumping up onto the stage.

We're stunned! He's pleased?

"Our last rehearsal was a disaster only because someone didn't bother to turn up. When a show works, it is because everybody works together. No one is more important than anyone else. The show is all that counts, and everyone has to serve it. I cannot afford any more dropouts. We have only two weeks left." He is looking straight ahead. "No one must ever miss a rehearsal again. Is that clear? Next time it will be different. Take this as a final warning to everyone. All I care about is loyalty to *iSezela*. Anyone who falls short of this, or does anything to jeopardize the show, anything, will bear the consequences."

Mosake locks each one of us into his gaze. Finally he stops at me. I see a warning in his eyes, and I try to hold his stare. I can't. I know I was wrong; I drop my eyes.

"Next time, the crocodile will be fed. Do you understand?"

I feel a shot of relief, a spark of joy, and a shiver of dread at Mosake's final words. He means what he says.

There are murmurs of agreement. I let out a sigh, and catch Nongeni's eye. She winks at me.

"So, we understand each other. Good. Now, listen carefully while I give you these notes. Tisha, I want you to start with the first verse, and then, Sipho, you must repeat what she's saying before Gloria comes in . . . and Seraki, don't be so eager. You cut in too quickly. Slow down. You all got going too fast and that's why you dried up."

Mosake patiently gives us more notes and we start again, from the top. The musical's taking shape. I can feel it becoming tighter, slicker, polished. We're working together again, and the buzz is the same as it was before.

Our rehearsal is much longer than usual. And now Gloria is watching me. I've never noticed her looking at me like this before. Maybe she's interested. I will not let her see that I know, or that I am interested in her. Not yet.

Finally we finish and she comes over to me.

"I'm glad that you came back, Seraki," she says. She touches my arm.

"Me too," I say, and then Nongeni, Sipho, and Tisha walk over and join us. "Thanks, Nongeni."

"That's okay," she says. "For a moment, I thought we were going to have another screaming session."

"He's like that: Fire and thunder one minute, and the next as cool as if nothing had happened," Tisha comments.

"It was a good rehearsal in the end," I say, feeling awkward. I can't keep my eyes off Gloria.

"Well, I must fly," she says. "See you all tomorrow." She picks up her bag and runs out the door.

Through the window we watch her climb into a waiting car. The man at the wheel drives off with her.

"I think that's her brother," Nongeni says.

"More like her boyfriend." Tisha laughs.

We stand around. Without Gloria, the company seems different. "Well, I must be going too." I have nothing more to say. Can that man really be her boyfriend?

"I can give you a lift, if you like," Nongeni offers.

"Thanks. I prefer to run."

"See you tomorrow," Sipho-Smiler says, and the others wave to me. I leave the hall knowing I was rude to Nongeni. I have to stop doing that. She's my friend, and so are the others. They were happy to have me back. I start running, feeling for the first time in my life I really belong to something.

"Mr. Nzule, can I talk to you for a moment?" It is the day before opening night, and I have to tell him about the musical. I've been putting this off for long enough.

He's outside in the backyard, working on our primus stove. If it isn't cleaned regularly it doesn't work right. I hate it when I have to do the cleaning, but now that he's doing it I won't have to and I can talk to him. Talking with Mr. Nzule always goes best when he's busy doing something. He's very good with his hands and

81

proud of being able to fix things. He looks up from where he's squatting and grunts.

"Pass me the paraffin, and bring me a rag from the kitchen."

I get what he wants and squat down opposite him.

I have to get it over with. Ma hasn't told him yet or he would have said something. I want him to know that I'm not getting into trouble every night when I'm late like this. I have to tell him about the rehearsals and our show, and how much I want him to be at the opening.

"I want . . . ," I say, not knowing quite how to begin. "Could you come somewhere with me tomorrow night? There's something I want you to see." I wait for his answer.

"What?" He grunts again, as he mops up what's overflowed.

I'm not sure he's even heard me, but I go on. "It's a kind of a play—a play with music and songs. I'm singing in it."

He looks up.

"You're what?"

"I'm singing in a play. The director is Mr. Mosake and he wants me to invite you. Actually, he's asked all the parents to come. It's the opening night tomorrow. It's very good and I think you'll like it."

Now that I've got it out, I can't stop babbling on about Cathy, the songs, the crocodile, Josh, the other kids . . .

He puts down the primus stove and looks at me.

"Hold it! Slow down. You're in a musical?"

"Yes."

"Since when?"

"We started rehearsing weeks ago. I didn't think it was important enough to tell you about before, but now I'd like you to come—if you want to. Ma's still trying to get the night off . . ."

"Your mother knows?"

"Yes."

"Okay, I'll come."

"We've worked very hard. Mr. Mosake says we're better . . ." I stop. "What did you say?" I have to make sure I heard what I heard.

"I said I'd come."

"You'll come?" Mr. Nzule says he'll come!

"Thanks, thanks a lot!"

He's not angry! He's coming.

Sometimes I don't understand Mr. Nzule at all.

"FREEDOM LIKE A RAY . . ."

Backstage, the dressing room buzzes with excitement as we get ready for our big night.

"Somebody, zip me up the back."

Everything's in place. Everything's ready. Everything's the way it should be.

A button comes off.

"Cathy, help!"

In a corner one of the girls is going over and over her lines in a desperate mutter. She's making me nervous.

"Can't you do that somewhere else?"

"Where do you suggest, Seraki?"

"Anywhere! I don't care. In the toilet!"

Josh comes rushing into the dressing room.

"Now, all of you. Don't forget the new words at the end: 'Freedom like a ray . . .' " He shouts to make himself heard over the noise.

"Like a fire burning. Like a burning light," we all chant back to him.

He checks through his notes, calling them out to us. We only half pay attention. We have to get ready; there's still so much to do.

The audience is arriving. Outside, the car park is full. We hear voices in the street, laughter. I peer through the window and see people strolling up to the Community Center.

Cathy comes running in with a needle and thread.

"Who's lost a button?"

"Cathy, over here! And look what I've done. I got makeup on my silk dress," Gloria says, almost in tears, as she tries to wipe the smudge off her party dress.

"A bit of water will fix that. Here, turn round."

"This is your ten-minute call, everybody. Ten minutes."

Ten minutes! I can't believe it. In ten minutes we'll be out there on the stage in front of all those people. Everyone will be looking at us, waiting to be impressed.

What am I doing here? Dressed in my school uniform, makeup on my face, and warming up my voice. Will I remember everything?

Mosake comes into the dressing room. He's calm, smooth, dressed in black and white. He wears a bow tie, a cream scarf over his shoulder, and his soft hat placed firmly on his head. In his buttonhole is a red carnation. He looks sharp.

"You knock them dead tonight. Knock them dead, do you hear?"

"Yes, sir!" we chorus.

Shoo! Am I excited!

I feel as if my blood's racing around twice as fast as usual. I want to piss all the time. Instead of butterflies in my stomach, I've got vultures!

"Anyone seen my police hat?"

Tonight Sipho-Smiler isn't smiling. He's searching frantically, all over the dressing room, bumping into everybody.

"Hey, watch it!"

"Sorry! I got to find my police hat."

"There it is, Sipho, look over on the costume rack."

"Stand by, please! This is your stand-by call."

We file out of the dressing room and move toward the stage.

In the dim light of backstage the eyes of the crocodile gleam red. Mosake has carefully placed it so that we can each touch it

84

on our way to the wings. I pass my hand over the scales on its back.

Make it magic tonight, iSezela, make it magic.

We stand, wait, and listen to the noise coming through the curtain. It's the sound of a large, restless animal.

"They're hungry out there tonight," Gloria whispers.

A full house—there's not an empty seat.

My father's there. My mother and Phakane should be out there waiting, too, but they're not. My mother could not get the night off from her madam. And Phakane is sitting locked up in a cell.

Are you listening to the scorpions scratch under your bunk, Phakane? Are you staring through your square at moonlight?

Someone trips over a stage weight.

"Ouch!"

"Shhhh!"

The houselights go down. The animal becomes quiet.

The stage lights come up.

There's a silence of many people, waiting.

They wait for the stage to come alive.

We wait for our cue.

I must push Phakane to the back of my mind. I turn to Nongeni. "Nongeni, are you all right? You're shaking."

"Of course I'm shaking! I'm terrified, Seraki."

"Concentrate—that's what Mosake says we have to do. Concentrate all the time. Think of nothing but what you're doing. Everything else will take care of itself," I say, more for myself than Nongeni.

Why do I have the opening line? I don't want to go out there first. I'm going to forget everything . . .

"Go, Seraki!"

I run—fly!

The lights dazzle me. I can see nothing.

There's no audience out here, only a darkened hall, bright lights, a spotlight, Josh at the piano, and the sound of a breathing animal.

My fist rises to punch the sky.

I shout the first line.

"We're taught what you want to teach us. We learn what you want us to learn. But we cannot live as you want us to live!"

The school yard comes alive with students arriving at Soweto High School. They jump over dustbins, tumble down the aisle shaking hands with members of the audience, scramble up onto the stage, and start chanting. "No trouble, only education." It is our first song. One by one, the characters are introduced to the audience. We dance, jive, bump across the stage until Nongeni, dressed as one of the teachers, comes in and tries to get order in the class. She teaches us biology. Today we are learning about reptiles: Crocodiles are her subject. We sing about the reptile, about its teeth, how it kills its prey, how it watches us, how it lives all around us. The biology lesson is interrupted by one of the boys, who rushes in and tells of the riot police moving into the township.

Sipho-Smiler, dressed as a policeman, comes charging in. Boys as dogs snap at our heels. We cower on one side of the stage, as the dogs are let loose. A smoke canister is exploded and we scatter across the stage. Someone throws the canister offstage, the dogs take off their collars, Sipho-Smiler takes off his too-big hat, and we step forward and sing about the crocodiles in our own lives.

After school we escort one of the girls home. She is afraid of her father, because she always fails her exams. He has warned her that this time she must pass or he will take her back to the country. Her father is always drunk, and if he catches her without a book in her hand, or not studying, he beats her. She sings about wanting to be free of her father, and how her parents don't understand her. When she finishes, we apologize to the Future.

"What can we say to the future . . . ?" leads us into the future song. As the lights go down, we move to the exam scene, where we are all writing our tests.

The musical is just like all the times before. Except that now it's perfect!

The performance moves from one peak to the next. We're riding on a giant force that pushes us higher and higher. After each number the audience applauds. We've never been applauded before. We're not used to it. Sometimes we continue on too soon, before the clapping dies down. Backstage we frantically change costumes. No one says anything. We think only of getting to the end of the first half.

Interval's come and gone, and we're back on stage. We're more confident than ever and our singing gets better and better. We are so well rehearsed that we start enjoying ourselves. Our mood is contagious, and the audience claps louder and longer after each number.

It's so different with an audience. They are giving us life, breathing fire into *iSezela*, supporting us with their enthusiasm. They laugh where we don't expect it, clap where it wasn't planned, and shout supportive comments all through the evening.

In the second half, our class is in progress when the gangsters come in and kidnap Gloria from her desk. Sipho-Smiler and I try to stop them, but they beat us to the ground as they grab Gloria and shove her out of the classroom. Teddy, the teacher, carries on teaching as if nothing has happened. Eventually he is bundled out of the classroom and we stand together to sing the jackrolling song.

> How can we learn
>   when we are not safe?
> How can we grow
>   when we are threatened?
> Who will protect us
>   from the terror of these men?
> What chance do we have,
>   if we do not stop this evil?
> iSezela, we are watching you
> iSezela, your time is over!

As we finish, the audience is quiet. It is a stunned silence. And then they erupt into applause, cheering, and shouting. We stand, waiting for them to finish, and then we carry on. The boys get together and plan to rescue Gloria from the gangsters.

We steal some tear gas from the police station, and throw it through the window of the gangsters' den. The boys rush in to rescue Gloria. They come out victorious. We dance to celebrate

Gloria's freedom. Sipho-Smiler runs in with the news of the exams we have written. We wait as he reads out the results. One by one, we jump and do a jive and a twirl around the stage. We have all passed. There is a way out of this ghetto life.

We've reached the final moments of the show. Josh pounds away at the piano; sweat runs down his face. We have angels in our voices. We have sung the roof off. We are singing to the skies.

We line up for our final bows and the audience is clapping, stamping, cheering. They won't let us finish.

We take bow after bow.

We sing the last song again, and again, and again.

They still won't let us finish!

The curtain closes for the last time. We look into one another's faces.

What have we experienced together tonight?

We gather on the stage and hug and pound one another.

I catch Gloria's eye. She moves toward me in the crowd, squeezes my hand, and whispers something in my ear. I can't hear her, but before I can ask her to repeat herself, she slips out of my embrace.

Mosake appears in the wings. With one mind we flow to surround him and lift him high above our heads.

We want this moment to last forever, to carry Mosake above our heads forever.

"Well done! Well done, everybody! You're all my stars! All of you! You're all my stars!" Mosake shouts down at us.

We've pleased him.

He's happy.

Nothing else matters.

THE BIG APPLE

Mr. Nzule slaps me on the shoulder and shouts to everyone in the shebeen, "Here sits the next Michael Jackson! You should have seen my son sing and dance tonight, just like on the television! What a voice!"

I can't remember ever having been so happy.

Auntie Somoza puts a round of drinks on the table, a heavy arm on my shoulder, and a wet kiss on my cheek. She winks at me. Who would have thought that I'd be sitting in her shebeen on a Friday night—with Mr. Nzule—celebrating!

"You should have been there! I tell you, my son, like a movie star!" Mr. Nzule shouts again to the whole room. Somebody cheers. He slaps me again, and gives me the closest thing to a hug I've ever had from him.

After the performance Gloria turned around and kissed me—I mean really kissed me, man! Right in front of everybody. I looked into her eyes and then drew her outside, and she didn't resist. Once we were alone she reached up around my neck and kissed me again. This time it was longer, and we held onto each other as if everything else around us had stopped moving. We couldn't stop kissing and my tongue moved in and out, saying hello to her tongue, and she bit my lips, and said howzit to my tongue, too, until we both ran out of breath, and we pulled apart and looked at each other. She said I was fantastic: I love you, she said. I said nothing—I couldn't! I've never felt so terrific and now, to be with Mr. Nzule, like this, in Auntie's shebeen . . . !

I've never seen Mr. Nzule so happy. After the show he came backstage and said he wanted to take me out to party. Everybody else was planning a celebration in the hall, but I wanted to go with my father. I had never been to a party with him before, never seen him like this.

And here we are at Auntie Somoza's!

"You've made your father proud," Auntie Somoza says, grinning at me.

I nod and smile back at her; I can't say anything. I'm too amazed, too proud, too jump-up-and-down-happy.

"Good! Your father needed something to cheer him up. You did good."

I nod and grin at her again. I only wish my mother and Phakane could have been there.

"Funny boy!" She laughs as the door opens and King Danny comes into the room. He stands for a minute with his men behind him, peering through the smoke. People look up at him, and then carry on talking, but not so loudly.

I want to disappear. He mustn't see me!

Too late!

He comes over to us.

"Everyone having a good time, hey?" he says, leaning across the table. "You got that money you promised me, boy?" he asks, ignoring my father.

"How do you know my son?"

"Ask him! I need the money, boy! Phakane's been moved. It's going to be more difficult to track him down."

I feel Mr. Nzule's eyes on me.

No, this can't be happening!

I make a dash for the door, but King Danny's too quick for me. He puts out his foot. I trip, fall, bang my head against a table. I remain on the floor. My father leaps up and punches King Danny. Danny's men pile onto my father and pull him away from their boss.

"It was stupid to try that, boy." King Danny grabs my shirt and pulls me up to him. "You want to see your brother again? You owe me money. We had an agreement."

"What agreement?"

"Nothing to do with you, Nzule."

"Leave my boy alone!"

"You shut up!" King Danny walks to where his men are holding my father and punches him in the stomach. "I'm not talking to you!"

I stagger up, my father goes down, and Auntie Somoza uses all her weight to hold back King Danny.

"Somoza, don't be smart. Shebeens are very easy to burn down. Be careful, Auntie." She moves away. Her clients have disappeared. Nobody wants to get mixed up with King Danny.

"Phakane's been moved to another prison," he says. "I don't know which one, yet, but if you come up with the rest of the money I might get you in to see him again, and maybe, just maybe, arrange his release."

He yanks my money pouch from around my neck and opens it and takes out the notes.

"Fifty-two rand only? Well, it's something. You do want your brother out, don't you?"

My father is coughing and gasping.

"Sorry to spoil your party," King Danny says to no one in particular, and snaps his fingers at his men. They drop my father and follow him out the door. The room is quiet, except for my father's heavy breathing on the floor.

He looks up at me.

"You've been giving King Danny money?"

"Yes."

"Where did you get it?"

"Mosake pays us."

"How much?"

"Seven rand a rehearsal and ten rand a performance."

"Bloody fool!"

He's on his feet now and slaps me hard across the face. It's unexpected, and painful. My head rings, and Mr. Nzule leaves without saying a word.

* * *

We are getting ready for another show. A week has passed since that night with King Danny and Mr. Nzule. At home everything is uncomfortable again. One moment Mr. Nzule is angry, and the next my mother is crying for no reason. My parents seem to feel that Phakane has come back into the house without really being there. And I am the one who brought him back. His memory sits on my shoulder, and every time my mother looks at me, she must see Phakane. Every time Mr. Nzule comes home, I think he hears Phakane in my voice. We are back to those days when the police came and took him away.

And everyone has heard about what King Danny said to Mr. Nzule, to Auntie, and to me. We are touched with the smell of the Naughty Boys. Nobody knows us anymore. We smell of trouble.

Nothing is ordinary. The only thing that is regular is the musical. Every night I escape to the performance, where there is no pain, sadness, hate, or tears. At the theater there is only bright lights, music, laughter, and loud clapping. Every night I run to the auditorium, get dressed, do a warm-up with Josh, perform, come home. Every night I do the show, and each time it's the same, but not quite, because each time I get better at it. And each time I feel freer, stronger, happier, until I get home.

Mr. Nzule is fighting with me, my mother is fighting with him, and I am stuck in the middle. The only thing they agree on is that I am never to see King Danny again.

Tonight the show is sold out and the noise of the people entering the hall filters through to our dressing room. Josh is giving us notes. I am not paying attention. I don't understand why we have to keep on hearing what went wrong all the time. What about what went right?

"Remember to allow time for applause after the 'Freedom Like a Ray' number," Josh says, reading from his little book.

"Still more notes?" Tisha groans. "I thought we were perfect!"

"No such word, my little songbirds. No such word, in my vocabulary, or in Mosake's," Josh declares, as he continues giving us his endless notes.

I dress slowly, taking off my street clothes, putting on my school uniform costume, trying to block out Josh, Sipho singing at the top of his voice, Nongeni warming up in the passageway, and the other kids dashing around the dressing room as if it's opening night all over again. I want to think about the show, but my mind keeps returning to home.

After that night at Auntie Somoza's I had to tell my parents about my visit to the prison. My mother cried—not because she was angry, but because she was pleased to hear about Phakane. She kept asking me questions that I had trouble answering. I could not tell them Phakane's idea about the hunger strike he wanted to begin. That was the one thing I wanted to tell them, but he made me promise not to. I wish Uncle was here—I would tell him everything and he would know what to do.

When I told my parents about the money I still owe to King Danny, Mr. Nzule went silent. He looked hard at me and then at my mother. Then she handed him her purse and he gave me the rest of the money.

"You must pay off King Danny and have nothing more to do with him," he said.

I nodded.

"And you are to come straight home after every performance."

I said I would.

"And give all your singing money to me."

I agreed.

"And it could be very dangerous for you to try to see Phakane again."

I said I know.

But what Mr. Nzule doesn't know is that when I paid King Danny for the last time, I gave him a note and asked him to slip it to Phakane. I couldn't leave my brother wondering why I was not coming again.

"Seraki! You're not even dressed yet! Come on! It's five minutes before curtain." Sipho slaps me on the back and shakes me. I've been staring into the mirror, not doing anything.

Why didn't Mr. Nzule understand? What is wrong with wanting to see my brother, and trying to get him out of prison?

"Seraki! Come on!"

"I'm coming, I'm coming!"

"They're going mad out there waiting for us. Everyone wants to see *iSezela!*" Sipho says, dragging me out of the dressing room while I button my white shirt.

As we move toward the wings, the crocodile waits for us to stroke its spine like we've done every night since our opening. Its eyes glint red in the dark. It watches over everything we do.

I wish it could help me.

In the wings Gloria gives me a squeeze. "I've got something for you, afterward," she whispers, leaning forward and blowing gently into my ear.

"I can't. I have to go home. Maybe tomorrow night," I say, and move quickly away so I won't see the disappointment in her eyes. I've more important things to worry about than Gloria. Life has become more complicated since I jumped on a truck and followed that red sports car.

Once the show starts the only thing I can think of is the music and the movement. For almost three hours I become somebody else and I don't worry about Uncle, Phakane, my parents, King Danny, or myself. In those three hours we blast off into the skies, away from our normal lives, and everything becomes bigger and smaller. Everything is either alive or dead, everything is bright or black. And the audience drops their fancy ideas, leaves their troubles at home, and comes with us. Nobody gets left behind. We take everybody with us on our rocket-ship ride.

After the show Nongeni's father gives me a lift some of the way home. We've been doing this since the second performance. Her father is stiff, proper, and polite. He drives his car carefully, slowly, avoiding all the potholes. I know this makes Nongeni mad.

Usually we talk about the show and what happened that night. Tonight nobody is saying anything. Nongeni is upset because her father is on her back again about her future. He is a doctor and wants her to be a doctor or a lawyer, not someone who sings and dances in musicals.

Nongeni is looking out the window, but I know she is not seeing much of this better part of the township. Here there are new houses, high fences, polished cars parked in garages bigger than my house. And everything is lit by electricity. No paraffin lamps and shadows here.

Her father looks straight ahead, but every now and then I see him glance at me in the rearview mirror. "What do you want to do with yourself after you finish school, Seraki?" he asks. The question catches me. It's one of those conversations I try to avoid. I never know what to say, and I can see by the way Nongeni moves her head that she is waiting for my answer too.

"My father doesn't really care what I do. As long as it makes money," I answer.

"But what do *you* want to do?"

It's not as if I've never thought of this before, but it's always been dreamy sorts of things: a soccer player for Kaiser Chiefs when I was younger; a leader of a political party when Phakane was around; a racing-car driver when I drove into the country; a member of a band when Uncle came visiting. All of them were childish thoughts, foolish things you can't say out loud to a serious adult like Nongeni's father.

"I mean, do you want to be a lawyer, a doctor, a businessman . . ."

"I want to make money and change things," I say, not knowing where this sentence comes from, but realizing with a little shock that that is what I want. It doesn't matter what I become, only that I change things—like how my parents live, like how Phakane got into prison, like stopping the Naughty Boys. There are so many things to change.

"Very sensible, but change what?" Nongeni's father asks, smiling at me in the rearview mirror.

"I don't know," I say, but I do know, and I'm not going to explain it to this man who's looking at me like I'm a child. "You can drop me off here," I answer.

He pulls over and I get out of the car.

"I'll see you tomorrow, Nongeni."

"Get me there, Seraki!" she calls after me as the car pulls away.

I feel light and comfortable out on the street again. Running home, I think about changing things, about buying dynamite, about clearing all the people out of the township and blowing it up. Then I will build new, clean white houses with gardens, and office blocks with green parks, and schools with playing fields. I don't know how, but I'll do it. I will change things.

Three nights ago Fat Oswald got his nose bloodied and was thrown out of the show. I was backstage, and saw Mosake punch him in the face. Cathy was there, and so was Sipho. She tried to stop him, but she couldn't. I think she may have been crying.

There was angry shouting, and a lot of blood, but Tisha, Gloria, and Nongeni only got there in time to see Mosake chase Oswald out the side door. Sipho said fat people bleed more than other people, and from the mess on the floor, I think he's right. There must be more blood in fat people.

When Mosake turned around and saw us watching him, he shouted at us to clean up the blood and get back to our dressing room. His fists were clenched and the skin around his mouth was tight. His eyes were red, too, and I thought of the glint in the crocodile's eyes.

We've seen him angry before, but never like that.

Later, Josh told us that Oswald was dropped because Mosake doesn't need his money anymore. The show's making enough money on its own.

Naturally the whole cast heard about it, and we were quieter than usual when Mosake came into our dressing room. But he was smiling. "What's the matter?" he said. "You all look so worried! Oswald was trying to take more than his fair share, and I can't let him have your money, now can I? He was only part of the show for the first season. Now that we have extended the run for another two weeks, it's none of his business. We've all worked hard for this success and I'm not going to let someone take advantage of you. Besides, making money is hard work and nobody can afford to throw it away. But Oswald's gone now and we won't be seeing him again. I'm looking after you and, in return, I want to see your best performance ever. There are some very important people in the audience tonight.''

And once again he was the Mosake we know, and soon he had us all laughing with him and we forgot about Oswald. He probably got what he deserved.

We haven't seen Fat Oswald since that night. We haven't seen Mosake for ten days now. Everyone is wondering where he is. There's a rumor that he's negotiating with the television people. I don't believe it. I doubt that the South African Broadcasting company would ever allow this musical on national television.

But even without Mosake, everything has gone along smoothly and we've played to full houses every night for the last three weeks. My mother finally came to see the show and afterward she was so excited she hugged me right in front of the others. She kept saying over and over how she wished Uncle could have been there. He could have easily come to see me on the stage, if he'd stayed around. Instead, he ran away again. I'm beginning to think he runs away a lot, but of course I can't say this to my mother.

For two weeks I've been hoping to get a message back from Phakane, and I can't help wondering if King Danny threw my note away. I've been looking out for King Danny, despite my father's warnings. But I can't ask anyone about him, not even Auntie Somoza. They might tell my father.

At interval Cathy comes rushing into our dressing room.

"Tonight you're all to stay on stage after the show," she orders. "We've something important to tell you!"

"Such as what?" asks Gloria, slowly turning so that she can see herself in the mirror.

"Wait and see!" Cathy answers, smiling, and rushes out.

"It's the return of the Great Pig," Sipho-Smiler says, impersonating Oswald. We all moan together before we race back on stage for the final act.

The curtain comes down, the applause dies, the audience leaves, and we mill around, waiting and wondering what that something important can be.

When Mosake comes striding onto the stage, we know from the serious look on his face that it must be something really important. He walks among us, not saying anything, looking very severe. "How would you like to go to New York?" He lets the words sink in. "The Liberty Globe Theater there has asked us to bring our musical to Broadway." We stare blankly at him. "Do you hear me? We are going to New York!"

We can't take it in, and can only stare at Mosake and watch Josh and Cathy hug each other.

One of the boys lets out a yell, and then everyone is talking and yelling at once.

"We're going to America . . ."

". . . to New York City . . ."

". . . where Bill Cosby lives?"

Suddenly everyone's jumping up and down—everyone except me.

Mr. Nzule won't let me go. And Phakane? I can't think about leaving while he is still in prison.

"Seraki, we're going to New York! Don't you understand? America! We're going to perform on Broadway!" Nongeni yells.

"What's Broadway?"

"Haven't you ever heard of Broadway? It's where all the big stars perform. Everyone knows about Broadway!"

"I don't."

Mosake takes a sheaf of papers out of his briefcase, and speaks. "We'll start rehearsing again tomorrow afternoon. We must make changes for an American production. And you must take these contracts home to your parents. Cathy's written in the dates of when we fly out of South Africa and open in New York. We leave South Africa on the fifteenth of November. That doesn't give us much time to rehearse a new show and prepare for our journey."

And again everyone's talking at once.

"I can't believe it . . ."

"New York!"

". . . flying to America."

"Now listen," Mosake says. "I want a meeting with your parents tomorrow night. I'll explain everything in detail then."

Nobody has ever been on an airplane.

Nobody has ever been out of South Africa.

And nobody has ever even dreamed of going to America.

This would be the biggest first of my life—New York City—and I hate firsts. But it's got to be better than staying at home with my parents, or hitching a ride on the back of a truck. This rocket ship, *iSezela*, has taken over my life.

And I'll be earning more money, which will help Phakane. If I go to America, maybe he won't have to go on a hunger strike.

I must let Phakane know.

I'm going to New York, to a place called Broadway.

CITY IN THE SKY

When I sleep I often dream of flying, like I'm falling from a telephone pole or a tall building or sometimes even from a mountain, but as I'm about to hit the earth my body suddenly knows how to fly, and, skimming the ground, I soar up into the sky. Without wings, I stretch my arms and turn from side to side, guiding the energy, and use my legs to go either up or down. I don't know where the power comes from and sometimes—if I allow myself to be scared—it's like being shot out of a cannon.

My flying is faster than the express train from Ikwezi Railway Station to downtown Jo'burg, faster than driving on the roof of Lucky's LookSmart minibus, in fact, faster than I've ever traveled before. My dream-flying is full of stomach-punching plunges, sudden swerves, and dizzy rolls. The flying is noisy, too, with the wind making my eyes water and my clothes flap.

This is what I imagined flying in an airplane would be like. But it was nothing like my dream-flying: It was boring and cramped, and it felt like forever. When we took off and the plane shook, we were pressed to our seats, and we left the gray runway behind. That part was exciting. We went over a shanty town and highways with tiny cars, and the bright blue puddles in other neighborhoods that Gloria said were private swimming pools. Sipho-Smiler said the large golden squares of sand were mine dumps. He said his father was down there turning the sand out of the earth in a mine just like that. Then he didn't say anything more and he didn't smile.

Once our airplane leveled out, not much happened. We were above clouds, above Africa, and all strapped into our seats, breathing stale air. After we changed planes in Europe, I kept trying to crunch my body to fit my seat for sleeping.

It was difficult telling my parents about the tour to America. My mother hugged me, pressed me into her breasts—which always embarrasses me—and said how proud she was of her son. Mr. Nzule sat, his elbows on his knees, his head bent, staring at a stain on the floor in front of him. He listened as if I were talking about the price of milk going up again.

I wanted him to smile, congratulate me, anything, but instead he said, "You do what you like anyway," and then after a moment, "You'll go whatever we say, so why are you asking us?"

"Don't you want me to go?" I said, trying not to sound angry.

But then he got up, grunted, and left the house.

It hurt worse when my mother cried. She said she would lose me forever and that I wanted to leave her. That wasn't true, but I had to tell her we'd be away over Christmas. Mosake said it could be anywhere from two to six months.

I didn't know if I wanted to go. New York is at the other end of the world, and I've never been away for such a long time. Gloria, Sipho-Smiler, and Nongeni all said it was an opportunity that could change our whole lives. That's what I was afraid of. I know what I am now, and I like who I am, and I don't know who I will be if I change.

But I worried about Phakane the most. We went back to rehearsing new bits for the show, and the preparations for the trip went on all around us. Slowly I became as involved and excited as everyone else. Then I didn't have time to think about Phakane. I was too busy learning new routines, fitting out new costumes, applying for a passport, shopping for winter clothes. We were even interviewed by the newspapers, and Auntie Somoza saw me on national news with the rest of the cast.

There was still no news of the hunger strike that Phakane said we would hear about, and I thought that perhaps he had changed his mind. In the end, however, even that wasn't enough to keep me from going to New York. I wonder if he would have done the same thing.

I spoke to Nongeni about Phakane. She said that we would earn more in one week on Broadway than we earned in two months in Soweto. And it would be in dollars, and with money like that I could hire the best lawyer in South Africa.

That idea helped, but still I felt as if I was leaving Phakane behind. I don't mean in South Africa, but leaving him behind in my head. He seemed to be getting smaller in my mind. The memory of his face and his voice was growing fainter, almost as if he were fading away. I asked Mr. Nzule to try and get hold of Phakane, but it was impossible. They had moved him again. They said we could write to him, but they never said if he would get the letters. And right now, as I sit on this jet plane halfway to New York, all those bad feelings have returned.

"Look at those two buildings! They're the same!" Tisha says, pointing at a pair of tall, slender buildings that pierce the gray-white sky.

"That's the World Trade Center," says Bob Haskins, the director from the Liberty Globe Theater. "They're two of the tallest buildings in the world."

After we took an hour to find all our luggage, and another hour to get through customs, Mr. Haskins, not Mosake, met us at the airport. He is the first American we met. He smiles a lot, talks loudly all the time, and slaps the boys hard on our shoulders. He's everything I expected an American to be: tall, blond, wearing a pin-striped suit, a trench coat draped over his shoulders, carrying a smart leather briefcase, and speaking like they do in the movies.

On the bus, I have to lean across Sipho-Smiler to ask, "Mr. Haskins, where is Mosake? Why wasn't he at the airport?"

"He's up to his pits in plotting your lighting, kid. Busy as all hell since he came into town. You know there's lots to organize, but he'll connect with you soon. Now, you fellas, you call me Bob," he says, and punches Sipho in the arm.

I've never seen so many yellow cars before, with little black and white squares painted on them. They're driving six abreast, bumper to bumper in both directions, either going flat out or braking to a crawl. We're inching over a bridge now and, down below us, the river is thick with big ships and slow tugs and little white boats making fast white waves. There is a man in the car next to my window. He's talking on a telephone! Everywhere there is something happening.

We're entering the city now—Manhattan, Bob Haskins calls it— and we stare around us at steam rising mysteriously from gratings in the roadway; canyon following canyon of sky-high, geometric-looking buildings; masses of people, all with someplace to go, moving up and down the streets; yellow cars weaving crazily in and out of the other traffic; police cars dashing past with lights flashing.

And noise! So much noise! Horns, sirens, radios, whistles, pneumatic drills, car engines, train engines, and the tic-tac-tic-tac of a million high heels.

Where do all these people come from? Who are they all? I thought Soweto was crowded!

Our bus pulls up outside the Hotel Wellington. Nongeni and I tumble down the steps into a pack of dogs: two poodles, an Alsatian, a boxer, three terriers, and two little white fluffy things, all tied to a young man, and pulling him along the pavement.

"Ai, he must like dogs!" Nongeni says, as she frees herself from the tangled leads.

"Oh, no," says Bob Haskins. "He's a professional dog walker!"

"You mean he does that for a living?" Cathy asks.

"Sure thing. Dogs got to get their exercise in this city, and everyone's got to earn his buck the best he can."

We are waiting beside the hotel going-round-and-round door, when a black man strides past and shouts, "Yo, cousins! Welcome to the center of the universe."

His friend joins in. "Watch out for the White Tiger. See you all in Central Park after dark!"

They disappear into the crowd, and we look at one another, not knowing what they're talking about.

A white man in a dark green soldier's uniform opens the go-straight-through door for us. I've never been inside a hotel.

We go into the big front room and stand and stare—at the huge glass light-fitting with hundreds of bulbs hanging from the middle of the ceiling, at the acres of thick carpet, and at ourselves gaping in the mirrors on the walls.

"Come this way, everyone," calls Cathy, pointing us toward another room.

"Are those the kids from Soweto?" someone at the reception desk says.

"Can't be," someone else answers. "They're too healthy."

Why shouldn't we be healthy? I don't like the way those people are staring at us. I'm glad there is a separate room for us.

"Hi, everyone. Welcome to New York," says a man walking in from that other room. He is also wearing a dark green uniform, and a funny, round cap on his head. "You want to know anything about New York, you come to me," he says, slapping his chest. "Arturo Meléndez is my name, but you must call me Arturo! And don't be shy. In New York City nobody's shy!"

He tucks a bag under each arm, picks up two more in each hand, grins at us, and goes out.

"Arturo's your main man here at the Hotel Wellington," Bob Haskins says to us. "He's a great guy. Now here's the score, folks. You listen to him and you can't go wrong."

Mosake strides into the room. Some of the girls whistle at the snappy sunglasses, smart black leather jacket, and expensive cowboy boots he is wearing. He looks more like a movie star than the Mosake we know, but it's a relief to see him anyway.

"Hi, everybody!" he says, as Cathy moves to be the first one to greet him. He kisses her briefly, and then in a very bad American accent says, "So, whadda'ya think of the Big Apple?"

We all laugh at him, crowd around him, admire his clothes, and try unsuccessfully to answer him with the same kind of twang.

"Ai, did my kids miss me?"

"Yes!" we all shout.

Cathy starts reading a list to tell us where our rooms are. "Tisha and Nongeni, you're on the twentieth floor, room 2020."

The twentieth floor!

"Seraki and Sipho, you're in room 2045."

"I'll never be able to sleep so far from the ground," Sipho shouts and everyone is talking at once.

We can't hear Cathy anymore. She tries to shout above the noise, until Mosake raises his voice. "Calm down, everybody. Calm down and listen."

We settle down onto the thick carpet and listen as he speaks. "I know you're all excited and everything is very new and strange. However, you must remember that we have come here to work, to work very hard. In two days' time we open in the toughest theatrical community in the world—Broadway."

"Two days!" gasp Josh and Cathy.

He stares them into silence before he goes on. "We have a lot to accomplish before opening night. No one may leave the hotel today or tonight. The city is not going anywhere. There will be plenty of time for you to explore, once our show opens on Saturday night. Now it is more important for you to rest and catch up with New York time. We begin rehearsals in the morning."

"Tomorrow morning?" someone blurts out.

"Yes. I've spent the last two weeks preparing for the next two days. You only have a day, a night, and a morning to rehearse on the stage before opening night. We are no longer in Soweto. We're in New York. The rules are different here. Only the fit and strong survive. Broadway will eat the weak and spit them out into the ocean. Saturday we open, and that performance must be the most spectacular ever."

We look around at one another. This Mosake is different from the man who danced with us at our last rehearsal in the community hall. I wonder if it has something to do with this jet-lag business? Or is it being in New York?

Cathy looks hard at Mosake and in the silence that follows his last words, she speaks. "I will organize for you to have supper in your rooms . . ."

Sipho-Smiler interrupts. "Don't you mean lunch?"

"Lunch, supper, whatever you want to call it, but don't forget your body clocks still think it's evening, not one in the afternoon. You're to unpack and after you've eaten, I want you to draw the curtains and sleep," she says. "Go to your rooms now. The lifts—here they're called elevators—are around the corner behind the reception desk. I will come and check on you later."

While the other kids get their room numbers, Sipho and I race out of the room and around the corner. He beats me to hitting the lift button. Our trip to the twentieth floor is a real rocket-ship ride. It is worse than taking off in any airplane. My stomach is left behind in the lobby.

We wander down miles of quiet, softly lit passageways that smell of soap, looking for 2045. Our room has two big beds, each with its own reading lamp, an air-conditioning unit with many dials and fancy knobs, and a gleaming bathroom. The bathroom has white tiles and mirrors and a counter with two sinks and drinking glasses wrapped in clear plastic bags, toothbrushes, soaps, little bottles of I don't know what, and tall piles of white fluffy towels, a pile for each of us.

In the corner of the room is a large television set.

"Thirty-four channels," Sipho shouts, switching from one

station to the next, from a church preacher, to a weather report, to American news, to a program about space, to a roomful of women jumping up and down to music in tight, bright suits. He sits on the edge of one of the beds, staring, listening to the twangs and drawls of the commercials about breakfast cereal, carpet-cleaning machines, soap powders. I pull back the heavy curtains to get a look at the city twenty floors down, but all I see is the side of another tall building close up. In the background I hear more adverts for running shoes, second-hand cars, hamburgers, deodorant, and chain saws.

"Dial our toll-free number, 1-800-555-0424, and this water bed can be yours. Aqua Dreamland: 1-800-555-0424, for this wonderful offer. Don't delay. 1-800-555-0424. Dial *now*. 1-800-555-0424. All major credit cards accepted."

There is a knock at the door. Sipho opens it and a man in a white suit pushes a table on wheels into the room.

"Room service for 2045. Hot dogs, hamburgers, french fries, slaw, and a can of Coke for each of you." He's talking real fast and staring at us staring at all that food. When we finally pick up our plates and start eating, he's still standing by the open door. "Ahh, never mind," he says, shrugging his shoulders. "Just set your dirties outside when you're done, and welcome to New York." He closes the door behind him.

We spread the food out on the beds and, without taking our eyes from the television screen, we start on our piles of food.

With his mouth full of hot chips, Sipho says, "Do you believe it, Seraki? We're in the United States of America, New York City, twenty floors up in the Hotel Wellington," and he swallows it down with a slurp of Coke.

"This tinned Coke tastes strange. What about yours?" I ask, reaching for my second mushy hot dog. I want to stretch out on this big, soft bed, but I lick the yellow mustard where it's oozing out between my fingers first. "Ai, and Soweto is a thousand kilometers away."

"Thousands and thousands of kilometers away, you mean," Sipho says, yawning.

I yawn, too, and stretch out on the bed, wondering why my body feels so heavy.

We both lie still. Soldiers in smart blue uniforms are galloping through rows of tents, shooting their long rifles at half-naked men with feathers on their heads. The tents burn, the women scream, and dead bodies lay scattered on the earth. A mother carries the bleeding body of her child and stumbles, weeping, shouting after the blue line of horsemen riding away from the burning Indian township.

THE LIBERTY GLOBE

New York is cold, colder than any early morning in Soweto or winter night in the high country of the veld. My nose, cheeks, and ears burn from the freezing air, and breathing in is like swallowing ice. The sky is a cloudless blue, but the sunshine is not warm enough to melt the thin brown layer that's frozen on the pavement since last night when it sparkled with rain.

Only two days ago the fiery sun of Africa bounced off the hot earth and made me wish the cooler nights would come early. Is this the same sun?

It seems like every second person is wearing a fur coat. None of us has brought enough warm clothes for this kind of weather, and by the time we get to the stage door—walking even two blocks is slippery work—we are freezing.

However, we soon forget about the cold, wintery day outside when we see the Liberty Globe Theater, which is as big as a soccer stadium. All morning we dash about on a tour of the theater, to the dressing rooms, from the stage to the wardrobe, from the orchestra pit to the sound studio, like chickens looking for our chopped-off heads.

Mosake was right. We have so many things to get used to here in New York, it's going to be a lot of hard work. The dressing rooms have lots of mirrors with light bulbs all around them and a whole team of white people telling us how to fix up our black skins to make us look better for the stage. Sipho doesn't like it when one of them starts putting makeup on his ears.

"Nobody's interested in seeing my ears, so keep your hands off me."

A lady in a white coat tells me to take off my trousers right in front of her. She says she's my dresser. Nobody's dressed me since I was a little kid. She gives me three new sets of costumes, and none of them fits.

"I never used to wear makeup and I don't see why I have to now!" Sipho shouts. I leave Sipho to fight it out with the makeup lady and go back up onto the stage with Teddy.

"You guys think this is a tea party! Get a move on, or I'll have your arses in a sling!" Big Joe, the stage manager, shouts at one of his crew. I quickly move out of the way of this short man, with eyebrows like caterpillars face to face on his forehead. He shouts all the time at everybody.

Josh is in the orchestra pit.

"Hey Josh, you warming up?"

"I'm not playing. I'm not playing a note, Seraki! I came all the way from Africa and they said because I'm not a member of some union I can't play a single note," he says, slamming his musical score down on the piano. There are tons of new instruments in the band and a band leader they call the conductor.

"Who's going to be playing all those instruments?" I ask.

"You'll find out at the sitzprobe this afternoon," Josh replies, and disappears out of the pit.

"What's a sitzprobe? Josh?"

During the lunch break we sit in the auditorium and eat a sandwich full of a funny meat called pastrami, which someone's brought us from the deli. Nobody knows what a deli is, but the Coke in the tall cups tastes better than the Coke from the tins we drank at the hotel.

"I have made inquiries about attending school while we are in New York and—"

"Oh Cathy, do you have to talk about school now?" Teddy groans.

"I promised your parents you would continue studying and that's what's going to happen. If you read the fine print in your contract it says you all have to carry on with your education, so don't give me any trouble, Teddy, or you'll be on the first plane back to Soweto."

"Rather tell us how much money we're going to be making," Sipho says, taking another bite from his sandwich.

"Okay, I wondered when somebody would get around to that. Each week one hundred dollars will be deposited into a savings bank for each of you. The rest of your salary, another fifty dollars each week, will be given to you in cash, for spending money. Mosake will provide your accommodations and one meal a day at the theater before the show."

"That's more than three hundred and sixty rand a week!" someone shouts, and hearing that, everybody gobbles lunch and is eager to get back to work.

That's when we find out what a sitzprobe is. It is singing through the show with an orchestra, but without any movements. Singing our songs without dancing feels strange, and with a microphone stuck to my forehead I can hear my own voice echoing through to the back of my head.

After the sitzprobe we're up on the stage for our first full run-through. I try not to think about the day of that other first run-through, when I was late to the community hall. I don't think anyone remembers that day. I do. Mosake shouted then, and he is shouting now.

"Will someone tell me how our first lighting cue could have been wiped off the computer?" The auditorium is silent. "Will somebody speak to me?" Mosake bellows from the back of the theater. "Gloria, while I think of it, how many times must I tell you to enter from the upstage wings. Get it right, honey!"

"We only had one set of wings before," she answers back, and I know it's going to be a terrible rehearsal.

From that moment on, everything goes wrong: None of the lighting cues are working; the radio mikes keep coming off when we dance; we can't get used to the big stage; and Mosake keeps booming through his microphone from his seat at the back of the auditorium.

"Fill your space! Spread out! Gloria, follow the beat of the conductor."

Everything is too loud and none of us can get used to the new orchestra arrangement. Mosake sends Josh into the pit to play the piano. "I don't care about the unions! Just get into the pit and play the piano!" he shouts, but it doesn't help.

Sipho grabs his hat and *sjambok* from backstage and is shouted at by Big Joe. Somebody working up over our heads screams down at Big Joe. Then Mosake is out of his seat in the auditorium and comes up onto the stage and Big Joe shouts at him, "Get off my stage."

I am exhausted. Sipho is tense, and some of the cast members are close to tears. I want to tear off my costume and run outside, back onto the streets of Soweto, and trot home. The only problem is that it would be a long, long run and the way I'm feeling I don't think I could even walk back to the hotel.

"What time is it?" I ask Sipho.

"After midnight and we've been here since eight this morning."

"Clear the stage! The iron is coming down," Big Joe yells. "Setup crew, I want you here tomorrow morning at seven. Sharp!"

At last the run-through—more like a stagger-through—is over, and we move off the stage and into the wings. I'm still not used to how bright the stage lights are.

Mosake's voice, low and deadly, comes through the backstage speakers.

"I want the *iSezela* cast in the auditorium, now . . . before you get changed."

"Looks like the night isn't over for us yet," Nongeni grumbles, as we make our way through the pass door into the auditorium. This is going to be bad. Mosake is in a dark, dangerous mood.

We collapse into the soft theater seats and watch the iron curtain, a huge sheet of metal, slowly fall between the stage and the auditorium. The noise of the stage crew packing up to go home fades as the iron curtain drops onto the stage, and suddenly everything is very quiet.

Mosake walks down the aisles, stands in front of us, and folds his arms. "Back home people said I was crazy to take school kids to New York to perform on an international stage. They said I was sure to fail, that I was mad, that New York would never take to a South African musical. I'm starting to believe that maybe they were right, and that I am crazy," he says quietly.

Mosake is hot with rage. Don't look at him, I tell myself. He will burn you if you look at him. I drop my gaze and study the tiny bronze plaque on the back of the seat in front of me: THIS SEAT DONATED BY JACK HENRY WISECROFT, JR.

"You're all terrible! I've never seen you so uninvolved and stupid on the stage. What the hell is going on? Doesn't anybody know what they're doing? You are a lazy, pathetic bunch of snot-nosed kids who should have stayed in the township where you belong!"

It is a slap across the face, as hard as any Mr. Nzule ever gave me. We stare like dumb animals, unable to defend ourselves. Nobody moves, says anything. We are too tired, too hurt to react.

"Mosake, calm down," Cathy says. We haven't seen her since lunchtime. "We've all had a very long day. And the kids are barely over their jet lag. Can't you—"

"Don't ever interfere with my area, Cathy. Their performance is *my* problem! They are professionals now! They've got to behave like professionals," he says coldly.

Tisha starts crying.

"And tears aren't going to make any difference!" he yells.

"Mosake! That's enough . . . ," Cathy tries again, but is once more shouted down.

"In case you haven't noticed we are opening in New York tomorrow night. This is the United States of America, not Soweto, South Africa! The party is over. If you fail here, you are not worth anything anywhere. Do you understand?

"And no bunch of sniveling kids is going to have a successful show on Broadway. And success is why we are here. The only reason we are here." He pauses, his eyes roaming over all of us. His gaze falls on me; I look away. I am not strong enough to hold it.

"I want all of you here at six-thirty tomorrow, dressed, made-up, and on the stage by seven. We'll begin with another run-through, and it had better be an improvement on this evening's disaster."

He turns and strides up the aisle. Nobody moves until Mosake has gone through a swinging door into the lobby.

"Well, it could have been worse," Nongeni says to me.

"But the show is under-rehearsed," Gloria protests. "Our last rehearsal was a long time ago. How can he expect us to be as good as we were in Soweto?"

"Don't be stupid, Gloria," Sipho snaps back. "Nongeni was talking about Mosake's speech, not the brilliance of our performance."

"Some people are never happy," Tisha says, wiping her hand across her cheek.

"Listen, everyone," Cathy says, wearily getting up from her seat. "He doesn't mean what he says. You have to understand that he is as tired as you are, and under a lot more pressure. He's worked so hard to get this . . ."

Nobody stays to listen. We silently walk back to our dressing rooms to wash and change out of our costumes.

Outside the night is freezing. Small bits of white are falling out of the sky. Nobody but me seems to notice.

"Doesn't Mosake know that if he wanted the moon from us we would give it to him?" Nongeni says.

I look up at the starless sky. "The problem is that he doesn't only want the moon." I shiver as the wind cuts through my thin

112

jacket as we start walking back to the hotel. I am angry at Mosake. He is being unreasonable. In the back of my mind, this thought feels like a betrayal.

In the morning we eat our breakfast in silence, walk to the theater, put on our costumes and makeup. Sipho-Smiler isn't cracking jokes, Gloria isn't whining about her costume, Tisha and Nongeni aren't even gossiping. I keep to myself in a far corner of the dressing room, running my lines through my head.

On stage, we move around nervously. Mosake is sitting in the dark of the auditorium. His microphone is his weapon. On this brightly lit stage we are exposed and vulnerable. Every move we make we wait for the Voice to boom through the loudspeakers.

"Stop! Sipho, your line is too fast. How many times do I have to tell you?"

Sipho cringes, waves an apology into the dark auditorium, and slips behind some of the boys.

"Stop! That platform is not to be set center stage. Big Joe, where are your men?"

The crew hurries on stage, moves the platform, and slinks off into the wings.

"No, it's still wrong! More stage left. I want it center stage!"

This time, Big Joe directs his men himself and looks past the lights for approval. "More! That's it. Carry on."

We do the number again. Each time we hear the Voice, we squint helplessly into the dark. We can't see him, but his voice controls us.

"Come on kids, get it right," Big Joe whispers to us from his station by the prompt booth.

Even Big Joe seems nervous this morning. He's staying well out of Mosake's sight and silently encourages us. The stage crew watches from the wings and claps when we finish each number. Everyone is on our side against the Voice.

Sipho steps forward, says his next line, and this time we all breathe a sigh of relief when no booming comment comes back.

Finally, at two-thirty, we finish the run-through. With so many stops and starts, there's no way to know if we were any better than last night.

We sit on the stage while Josh gives us his notes. There's nothing we haven't heard a hundred times before. And there's still no way to know if Mosake is pleased. He left the theater straight after the rehearsal.

Walking back to the hotel, I'm lost in a blur of noise and movement. I am tired, and yet I can't stop thinking about tonight. Will these New York people understand our show? Are we ready? Can we be as good as we were before? Can I be better?

"I'm not hungry," I say to Sipho. "All I want to do is sleep."

I hope everyone else does the same.

"Thirty minutes," comes Big Joe's voice over the loudspeaker system backstage. Tonight, in thirty minutes, we open. "Thirty minutes to curtain."

Our final countdown has begun. Nervously we check this, re-check that, pacing aimlessly through space.

"Fifteen-minute call. Fifteen minutes to curtain."

Now we sit staring at nothing, until the familiar crackle of the loudspeaker comes again.

"Ladies and gentlemen of the *iSezela* cast. This is your five-minute call. Five minutes, please! Please assemble in the green-room," Big Joe broadcasts. "All cast members please go to the greenroom now." It must be part of a stage manager's job to say everything twice.

We leave our dressing rooms and file into the greenroom, which isn't green at all. It's dimly lit, with a single center light shining down on a table. Many Mosakes, in elegant evening suits, are reflected off the mirrored walls. We settle down to wait. My stomach wants to be anywhere else but here, and at the same time, nowhere else but here.

He steps into the light, takes the crocodile out of a bag, and places it on the table. The light catches its spine, its open mouth, and the red gleam in its eyes.

I have not thought about the crocodile since we left South Africa. Somehow I thought we'd left it behind, with everything else, back in Soweto. Now, it's strange to see it here, in New York. And comforting. If it brought us such good luck back in Soweto, then the crocodile will bring us the same luck here.

Mosake looks down at the crocodile and speaks. "We've come a long way together, from a township hall in Soweto to this theater on Broadway. Your crocodile has brought you here. You know that."

I nod. Next to me, Sipho murmurs his agreement.

"This is New York, and every one of you is about to be tested. That's why we came, to be tested on a stage where you will not be judged for your color, or by your background. Here you will be judged only by your talent. It will only be by your talent that you will survive." He pauses; his eyes pass slowly over us. "I can assure you that each of you has the necessary talent, but there is one question you must answer for yourselves: How much do I want to succeed?"

Mosake's voice is low and measured. In the mirror, I see Nongeni across the room. She looks terrified.

"If you want to be professionals, a great deal is going to be demanded of you. Everything here is more important than it was back home. This is a world where there is no excuse for failure. Did any of you come here to fail?"

Silently we shake our heads no, and Mosake nods his approval.

"We"—and he rests his hand on the crocodile before he goes on—"expect more from you than you have ever given before." The crocodile is grinning at us. Mosake smiles, lifts it from the table, and cradles it in his outstretched hands.

I am the first to understand his signal. I stand up and move silently past the others, until I am face to face with Mosake. Slowly, I run my thumb down the ridge of our crocodile's spine. I step aside.

Sipho comes forward and does the same.

One by one, we each stroke our crocodile.

"Now go, and succeed. Show them how wonderful you are."

We file out of the greenroom to our standby positions on stage. We hear the buzz and chatter of the audience filtering through the curtain. Big Joe signals us that he has received "front of house clearance." Our audience is seated and waiting for us.

Our conductor goes into the orchestra pit. Tisha is gripping my elbow, and together we watch the green lights flash on Big Joe's control panel.

The lighting operators are standing by.

The sound technician's light turns green. He is now standing by too.

High over our heads, in the dark behind the overhead spots, the men who work the flying scenery are also ready.

We are silent, tense, holding our breaths. Then the final signal comes. Big Joe whispers into his headset microphone, "Go, house lights."

The orchestra begins the opening sequence of our music. A hush settles over the audience.

We stand in the wings just as we did back home in Africa, on another opening night years ago and worlds away. Now the animal that waits restless behind the curtain is larger, stronger, more ferocious than the one we faced back home. Here our audience is not our family and friends. Will they understand us? Will they enjoy our music? What if we fail?

"Stand by, Light Cue one. Stand by, Curtain."

The curtain rises, the stage lights come up, the opening bars of our first number rise from the pit.

My fist punches the air.

I shout my first line: "We're taught what you want to teach us. We learn what you want us to learn. But we cannot live as you want us to live!"

The others join in, and we sing, lifting the roof off with our voices. A wash of sound rushes from the stage to the auditorium.

Nothing is different. We know what we're doing and we do it well. We draw power from the strange new audience sitting out there in the darkness of the auditorium, but they are no longer

116

threatening. They are our captives and we can do with them as we please. They must sit and listen to our story.

Everything's as it should be. We punch, jive, and sing our way through the first half, not allowing the audience a chance to breathe or clap. They are stunned; we are stunning. Gloria sings like she's never sung before; Sipho's comic timing is perfect; the dance routines are fast, energetic, and faultless.

We allow the audience to catch their breath during interval and then when we return we hit them harder with even better singing, better dancing.

Gloria is dragged out of the classroom by the gangsters and we sing our jackrolling song:

> How can we learn
>> when we are not safe?
> How can we grow
>> when we are threatened?

After the song is over the audience claps so hard that we cannot continue.

"Keep still," I whisper to the others. "Don't move!"

We freeze in our positions on stage and wait until the applause is over. It feels like we have been standing for five minutes before the applause dies down and we are allowed to go on. We have never had such a powerful reaction to that song before.

Our performances grow stronger and bolder as we reach the end of the musical. None of us wants the show to finish; we want to start all over again. But the curtain falls on the finale, and the people in the auditorium rise from their seats, clapping and shouting. The house lights go on and we see the faces of over a thousand people standing, clapping, cheering. I am struck dumb and stare back at all these people clapping for me, for us, for *iSezela*. We take our last bows, but they call us back, not even letting us properly leave the stage. We sing the finale again. We take call after call, until finally Big Joe brings the curtain down for the last time.

We rush into one another's arms and collapse in a heap on the middle of the stage, laughing, shouting, crying.

We've knocked Broadway right between the eyes!

"Where's Mosake?" Nongeni shouts above the noise.

I look around for Mosake. He should be here. We want to lift him above our heads like we did back in Soweto.

"Don't worry, you will see him later," Josh shouts back.

For a moment we stop our celebrating. It is not the same without Mosake here. Sipho looks at me. I shrug, let out a yell, and then race back to our dressing rooms to change for the opening night party that Bob Haskins promised us.

CROC SUPREME

"How can we eat anything so pretty?" Nongeni gasps, staring down at her plate.

My plate looks exactly like hers, with radishes sliced into the shape of rosebuds arranged around the edges. Spears of asparagus, like spokes of a wheel, with a red sauce center, lie under a neat square of—"It's fish," Mr. Quartermain, the man who introduced himself next to me, whispers in my ear—sprinkled with chopped nuts on a pile of lettuce. A quarter of lemon and a bit of green plant lie to one side.

The plate of food looks like a painting, with knives and forks lined up like soldiers protecting it from both sides. I don't know which fork to use, so I reach for a spoon. Mr. Quartermain nudges my elbow and points to his fork on the outside.

"Just put it into your mouth and don't worry how it looks," I say back to Nongeni, and hold up the fork a little too high so she can see which one we're to use.

"It all looks the same in your stomach," Sipho mumbles from his seat across the large round table.

* * *

We took our first taxicab ride to this Tavern on the Green restaurant in Central Park. Now that was a first I liked. Our driver sped through the park under the leafless trees strung with little white lights, blinking like they were dusted with magic.

Inside, the restaurant has mirrors everywhere, and chandeliers, and statues, and plants, and tall waiters in dinner jackets, and a band with rows of trumpet, saxophone, and trombone players. I've never seen anything like it! How Uncle would love to see those saxophones. How Auntie Somoza would love to run this place!

When we arrived everyone in the restaurant stood up and applauded us. It felt like we stood for five minutes before their clapping died down. We didn't know what to do, or where to look, until we were taken to our tables and shown our seats. Now, four of us are sitting between people we don't know. Across the room is a long table for Mosake, Cathy, Josh, Bob Haskins, and some other people I've seen at the Liberty Globe Theater. Big Joe isn't there, but I'm glad that Sipho, Gloria, and Nongeni are at my table. I wish one of them was right next to me, though. I'm not sure I'll be able to talk much to Mr. Quartermain.

"Who is that glamorous woman beside Mosake?" Gloria asks, turning to the woman beside her. I don't hear the answer, although her next question is clear. "Then those diamonds she's wearing are real?"

We both look at Mosake.

Cathy's wearing the same sequined black dress she wore on our opening night back in Soweto. She still looks beautiful to me. Mosake is not paying her much attention. I suppose Cathy looks ordinary in comparison to the Diamond Lady. She is wearing a white low-cut dress. She has long white gloves on, and her arms are laden with bright jewels.

The band strikes up, and some of the guests move toward the dance floor. Mosake speaks to the woman next to him. She smiles and rises, her hand in his. His hand is holding her waist, as he draws her to him on the dance floor. Cathy is watching them too.

We all whistle and cheer. I didn't know Mosake could dance so well. I look at Cathy. She's still sitting at the table, and gives me a wave and half a smile.

"That woman with Mosake is dynamite," I say to Nongeni.

She's watching Cathy talking quietly with one of the managers from the Liberty Globe Theater.

"I think she's overdressed!"

The music finishes with a flourish and all the dancers return to their seats. There's a fresh bottle of champagne on our table. Nongeni whispers that we're only allowed two glasses each. Already I've had four and feel like a bubble on a cloud. I've never been able to drink anything at Auntie Somoza's, and here I am sipping free champagne. No one back home will believe me when I tell them. Everything here is free, and this champagne's going to make polite conversation with Mr. Quartermain easy.

We've finished the fish, and now the waiter is giving us something that looks like ice cream in a tall silvery cup. Sipho looks worried, like this is the end of our meal, until the lady next to him says, "It's to clean your palate, before the main course."

The next plate is served and it looks like rump steak to me, even if it does have a fancy French name that Gloria seems to be getting a lot of mileage out of saying over and over again. I wonder if she also knows what a palate is?

After we have eaten, Bob Haskins comes over to our table, carrying another bottle of champagne. "Hey, kid," he says to me. "You've knocked New York right between the eyes. How d'you like this spread? Bet you don't eat like this back there in deepest darkest Africa."

I don't know what to say to that, but before I can think of something, he's talking again. "Now, before I hit you with the special bang-up finale I've ordered for this meal, you're gonna haf'ta sing for your supper. What d'ya say, folks?" He shouts past me, "Should we make 'em sing for their supper?"

He's answered by a tremendous cheer from all over the room, and Mosake nods to Josh.

We tumble out of our chairs and join him at the piano. "Okay, my little songbirds, let's get them where they live," he says, and nods at me as he hits the keys with our opening number.

I punch the air with my fist and shout my first line. The others join in, and we sing, punch, and jive our way through the opening number.

After our song is over the whole restaurant is on its feet, clapping, cheering, shouting for more. We turn to Josh. He is beaming. He calls us to him again.

"This time we'll get them where we live," he says, and plays the sad, sweet introduction to our jackrolling number.

For a moment, once the song is finished, our audience is silent. We have stunned them twice in one evening. Then they break into applause, calling for us to sing again. We look at Mosake. He is smiling. He is proud but jerks his head directing us back to our seats.

We want to go on. We want to sing and dance our way through the finale of our show, but Mosake rises to his feet and raises his champagne glass in a silent toast to us. Everyone else is on their feet, their glasses raised to Mosake, when Bob Haskins shouts, "You kids are the greatest!" The room erupts again in wild applause.

"You've made history tonight. New York has never seen a musical quite like yours. You've blown the socks clean off this Broadway season. You've surprised us all and in return we've got a whopping-great surprise for you."

He snaps his fingers and the waiters, with much ceremony, march forward and lay before us silver plates with chocolate crocodiles swimming in cream.

"I've called it the 'Croc Supreme,' " Bob Haskins shouts. "It's your iSezela that's gonna swallow this town whole, and tonight it's your turn to swallow the croc."

I look down at the marvel of chocolate in front of me. I don't like messing around with crocodiles, but everyone else seems to think it's a terrific idea. Sipho picks up his spoon and bashes his dessert in the head. As the cream splashes into his face, he laughs. I feel uneasy.

Crocodiles are too powerful to be joked with, to be made into chocolates floating in cream, to be eaten. Mosake places our crocodile where we can see it while we work. Our crocodile has been our good luck spirit, our judge, and sometimes our tormentor. It brought us here and it's nothing to be made fun of. Bob Haskins doesn't know that. How can any American know that?

I look across the room to see what Mosake's thinking. He's whispering into the Diamond Lady's ear and then he laughs loudly as, from his mouth, one of her earrings falls onto the chocolate fragment on his messy plate.

Cathy isn't in her seat on his other side. Her "Croc Supreme" sits untouched, looking up at Mosake.

And then in the middle of the night, the Sunday morning newspapers arrive, and I don't understand why great stacks of them are dropped on our table, and everyone is grabbing for them and falling silent as they read.

"Broadway Hit for Township Kids!!!" announces the headline on one of the pages of the *New York Times*.

" 'Nothing like the energy and dynamism of these young people from Soweto has ever before been seen on a Broadway stage. Quite simply, the show's stunning!' " Mr. Quartermain reads enthusiastically.

We cheer, and now we scramble to open the other papers. One rave headline follows another.

"New Broadway Opening a Must-see!"

"Township Cast Excels!"

"*iSezela* Sizzles!" makes us laugh.

"Imagine a sizzling crocodile!" Sipho shouts.

"Listen to what the *New York Post* says." Nongeni reads more good news: " '*iSezela* is a musical that bubbles with enthusiasm, humor, righteous anger, passion, and unquenchable hope. Do yourself a favor and go and see *iSezela!*' "

"Shoo, that's a lot of bubbling I didn't know about." It's Sipho talking as he leaps from his seat and leads us all in the *toyi-toyi* on the dance floor.

It is four o'clock in the morning when Bob Haskins announces another surprise. He's sending us back to the Hotel Wellington in horse-drawn carriages.

We pile into the five horse buggies waiting outside the restaurant. The coachmen tuck us up under thick warm blankets, and drive us off through the park.

The night air feels cold and fresh after the overheated restaurant. Around us the lit-up skyscrapers of Manhattan rise into the sky. Yellow street lamps glow and neon signs blink their many messages. High above, the few stars seem frozen, nothing at all like the warmth of those other stars that fill the sky over Africa.

NEW YORK TIMES

15 January 1990

Hey, Uncle,

It's funny to think that two months have passed since we landed in New York. Christmas and New Year have come and gone and we have performed *iSezela* 72 times! It feels like a year has gone by since I was last in South Africa. I was thinking of you today and then I got your letter—thanks. Everything's going much better now. I've got over the stomachache I told you about last time. I think it was all the junk food I'd been eating. Cathy found us a place that sells cornmeal, and so now we make our own *ipapa,* just like back home. It tastes the same, almost. The show's going well and we're still playing to full houses. There's talk of extending the run. We're getting a bit tired . . .

Since I've been in America I've started writing letters. Before I left South Africa, I had never written a letter to anyone. Now I write to Uncle, Phakane, my parents, and Auntie Somoza at least once a month. If you add it up that's one letter a week. I even wrote to Sweets and got a postcard from her. I like getting letters from home; whenever I write I always seem to get one back in the mail. I never thought I would get so excited about opening a letter with a South African stamp on it.

There's no letter from Phakane yet, but Ma says that soon there will be one in the post from him too. Six weeks ago he started his hunger strike and it lasted for twenty days before he was moved to a hospital. Now he can have visitors once a month. Mom says they are doing everything they can to get him released. They say he is very thin, but still talks as much as he always did. I think there is also a lot they are not telling me. When I get to those parts in their letters I wish I had never come to New York. Uncle sent me some clippings of the news regarding my brother's hunger strike. The papers don't mention him by name, but Phakane was right—the people have heard about the hunger strike. And I am not there—I am far away performing in a musical every night.

It's hard telling everyone back home about the people, the colors, the life and energy of this city. There are so many good and bad things here, that it's hard to make them understand everything. How can I tell them about the bad things without sounding ungrateful?

Like the weekends, for example. I'm beginning to hate Fridays and Saturdays. There are two shows on Fridays and three on Saturdays! Doing the show so often is tiring us out and by Sunday everyone's exhausted. I don't want to complain because it may sound like I'm whining or being lazy. After all, they'll say, you enjoy doing the show, and not everyone's given a chance like this . . .

. . . but I'm still enjoying myself. We are busy recording the musical. EMI has contracted a recording of *iSezela* and so every day we go to the studio to record. Of course, this doesn't give us much time for anything else.

I've always wanted to know what a recording studio looks

like. It's a large room with a microphone hanging from the
ceiling. We all crowd around the microphone and watch the
man behind a glass panel in the editing room. We also have
to watch the recording lights, and we each have earphones
to listen to the playback. It's very strange singing without
an audience. Bob Haskins says we must imagine we have
an audience, or we'll sound lifeless.

I put my pen down and look out of the window at the apartment
block across the street. Maybe there's something interesting going
on over there.

We were moved out of the Hotel Wellington a week after opening night. I think a lot of the kids thought that we were going to
stay there all the time, and were surprised when Mosake put us in
an apartment block on the Upper West Side of town. We still share
rooms. There are now four boys to one apartment, and each flat
has a small lounge and kitchen. It's not as comfortable as the hotel,
but it's still a lot better than home. The heater doesn't work as
well as at the hotel and we have to make our own food, but at least
we have a television set.

The weight lifter, who has the room directly opposite mine, starts
to work out with his pair of dumbbells. He poses, flexing his muscles and admiring himself in the mirror. Sipho and I call him Samson. The "purple" apartment, below his, is still empty. I wonder
who lives there? Apartment spotting's become a favorite game with
all of us. You can't help looking into somebody else's apartment
when the buildings are so close together. One afternoon we saw a
man beat up his wife with a golf stick. She threw books at him,
but that didn't stop him. Nongeni phoned the police, but it was too
late. The woman was taken away in an ambulance. The man was
taken away in a police car. There's not much action over there this
afternoon. Samson continues to sweat, and on the street below
students carry books to that big university that's all over this part
of town.

It's hot and stuffy in here; the heater is set too high. I open the
window and the blare of traffic rushes up and into the room on a
freezing blast of air. I shut the window. That's what I hate here.

125

You're always either too hot or too cold, and it's never quiet. Arturo says I have a bad case of the January blues. Everyone gets a bit ratty around this time of the year; he says it's normal.

I've made two very good American friends, Linda and Arturo. Linda works for the Liberty Globe Theater as a PRO—that means public relations officer. She's an African-American—that's what the black people here want to be called—and a feminist. She's very successful and runs the public relations office practically on her own. She takes Nongeni and me out to art galleries. She's also taken me to hear jazz. The other night after the show, Nongeni, Linda, and I went to the Blue Note, a jazz club in Greenwich Village. Uncle, you would have loved the sound those guys made. I thought of you.

Nongeni told me that one day she wants to be like Linda. She loves the way she deals with men: She doesn't allow Bob Haskins or Mosake to mess with her. Mosake doesn't like her; Linda doesn't like him either. She calls him the worst kind of chauvinist pig. He calls her that-woman-who-wants-to-wear-the-pants! Bob Haskins calls her a rampant feminist.

Nongeni and I were having coffee with Linda at a diner across the way from the theater one afternoon. Nongeni, who listens really carefully to everything Linda says, asked her why Mosake and Bob Haskins always give her a hard time. Linda laughed.

"They're just worried because I can do a job as well as they can, and that's something they don't want to have to believe," she said.

"And why shouldn't you do the same job they do?" Nongeni asked, sipping her milk shake.

"Because I'm a woman and women aren't supposed to be able to do the jobs men do. Not so, Seraki?"

I knew it was a challenge, and both the women looked at me, waiting for me to put my foot in my mouth. I shrugged.

"If you don't want babies then I suppose any woman can do a man's job."

126

Nongeni huffed at this. "Why does he also sound like one of them?"

"Because he's a sexist in training," Linda said, laughing at Nongeni's scowl and the casual way I sipped my coffee.

> Arturo works as a bellboy in the Hotel Wellington, and while we were staying there he showed me how to survive living in New York. Even now that we've moved out of the hotel I still go around and see him. He's a Hispanic-American and has lived all his life in New York. I found it strange when he said that he had never been out of the city. "This place has everything," he said. "Why do I need to leave New York?" I couldn't argue with that. Besides, his whole family lives in the city, and we are always bumping into cousins of his in the strangest places.

I think Uncle would like Arturo. He's more concerned about the Giants' football scores than American, or any other, politics. He works hard to save money, but then spends it all on his many girlfriends. I've seen him so angry with tourists who don't tip him that I thought he might beat them up with their own suitcases. And then I've seen him do an impersonation of Michael Jackson in the hotel foyer when no one is looking.

After the first month in New York, I was feeling completely worn out by all its noise and bustle. When I mentioned this to Arturo he said, "*Sí*, I understand—New York life's crazy life. Everybody's running around in circles and making everyone else dizzy. You want some peace, you come with me next Sunday. I'll show you some peace."

I forgot about our arrangement, but Arturo didn't, and come Sunday he took me to Brooklyn to meet one of his cousins, Alfredo, who works at the aquarium at Coney Island. We spent the afternoon at the aquarium, a quiet, green world of water and fishes.

"When I feel like I'm going mad, I come and watch the little fishies. They know more than you and I," Arturo said, leaning his face against the glass to kiss a fish that lazily yawned at us and then slowly floated away.

127

After that I've often gone to the aquarium and wandered past the tanks of tropical fish, allowing my mind to float away. I feel like going there now, but I don't have the energy to get off the bed.

I pick up my uncle's letter and reread some of his news. His letter is short, about a page of rough handwriting, and written on paper out of an exercise book. He wrote it in a hurry. With the letter are two articles torn from *The Sowetan*. One is about our success in New York. The other is about the hunger strike.

Uncle still hasn't been to my house since my father chased him away. He has joined a band, the Daring Hot Stix, and they play jazz every Saturday around the township. He has asked me for some money to buy a better sound system. He needs a thousand rand, which is about four hundred and fifty dollars.

It's hard to believe that five months ago I was in Soweto, hoarding my money in a leather pouch around my neck to pay King Danny. How important every five rand was! Over here it's worth nothing. In New York you can't buy a can of Coke for five rand. I'm getting used to the kind of money they're paying us here: four hundred dollars a month and fifty dollars a week, which Mosake gives us for food. That's six hundred dollars a month! It's difficult to stop converting dollars into rands. I'm earning almost fifteen hundred rand a month. My father and mother together don't earn that much! The others have been spending their money on dumb things like video recorders, clothes, and stuffed animals. I'm saving mine—not counting the food and books I buy and the movies I see.

I don't know what to do about Uncle. I have eight hundred dollars saved up since we opened two months ago. I want to give him the money and I don't want to. I am writing a long letter because I am thinking about what to say to Uncle about the money he wants to borrow from me. In the end I'll probably give it to him. At the moment he needs it more than I do.

You asked me what I do with my time off. Well, I don't
have much time to myself at the moment, what with the
recording sessions and everything. And Sundays in New York

128

are awful. Everyone is hanging around the Block—which is what we call the cement block of apartments we live in—and sooner or later someone is quarreling with someone else. That's why I like Arturo. He always finds things for me to do, and places to go on Sundays. He organizes what I call "Arturo trips."

We don't see much of Mosake. He's very busy. Cathy's always around in case we need her, and Josh looks after our performances and makes sure that the show remains in top gear. Cathy has organized school for us. You'll be pleased to know that I go to four classes a week at the St. John's Academy! School here is so different from South Africa. There are fewer pupils per teacher, and there are some very weird subjects: Community Psychology, Self-Awareness, and Futurist Studies! The last one is about coping with future shock, whatever that is.

Mosake and Cathy aren't going out together anymore. I feel sorry for Cathy: Mosake dumped her so publicly for that other woman. Linda says it's her own fault for allowing Mosake to walk all over her.

Sometimes it's hard to remember that Mosake's still got anything to do with the show, but one night Sipho forgot to make an entrance on stage, and the next day, sure enough, he was called in by Mosake. He got a real bawling out and some of his pay was docked.

In the apartment block across the street the Lady of the Plants has come in and is watering her ferns. She always wears the same apron and dangles a cigarette out of the corner of her mouth. Tisha has seen her on the streets digging through trash cans.

Uncle, thank you for the clippings from *The Sowetan*. Please let me know if you have any more news about Phakane. That part in the article about "prisoners being manacled to their hospital beds" was very scary. Are they allowed to do that to prisoners? Isn't there someone who can stop them? I need to know more about Phakane and feel very left out here. It's nice to know that we are remembered back

129

home. There's always something about South Africa in the newspapers over here, stuff we never hear about at home. Some of the kids are always talking about South Africa. I think they're homesick. I tell them that there's no point in missing home, because it's always there. I'm not homesick, but sometimes after the show I lie in bed and think of you playing your saxophone, or Ma cooking supper.

I think I might be a little homesick, but there's no point in telling him that.

The room's too hot again, but I'm just too lazy to do anything about it. I'm tired of writing. Maybe there's something on the television . . .

The phone rings.

It's Nongeni. "Hi, Nonsy, what's happenin'?" I say in my best New York accent.

"Cathy's leaving. She's going back to South Africa on the next flight."

"What!"

"She's leaving. I've been looking all over for you."

"Where are you?"

"I'm at the theater. Why aren't you?"

I look at my Rolex. A real Rolex, from a guy standing on the corner in Times Square. I paid fifty-five bucks for it and it's a real flasher. Big and heavy and all shiny gold. I know it's not real gold, but it looks like real gold. It says 4:52.

"Why are you there so early?"

"Early? It's five-thirty. You better get moving or you're going to be late."

It takes at least half an hour on the downtown subway to get to the theater. My watch must have stopped.

"Seraki, are you still there?"

"Yes, yes. I can't believe it. Listen, I've got to leave right now."

Cathy's leaving! That's a bad sign. I throw some stuff into my bag, check to see that the heater is still on, lock the three locks on the door, dash down the stairs, nearly tripping over a pile of newspapers on the second landing, and push through our security gate to the street.

I join the five o'clock rush hour into the entrance of the subway. My train to Times Square is there on the platform. It's a good thing I still have a token I bought from those kids that suck them out of the turnstiles and sell them cheap on the street. There's no time now to stand in the queue to buy a legal fare.

The train ride is taking forever. I hope there's not going to be the usual delays. They're always working on these tracks. A drunk lies curled up asleep in one corner, and there are several students at the end of the car. And a rap preacher is going on about the millennium.

Cathy can't leave. Who'll step in front of us when Mosake gets angry? Josh is not strong enough and he would never dare do what Cathy does.

Speeding through the dark tunnels, I remember the wind in my face that day I followed the red sports car to the Community Center and stumbled, bloody and sweaty, into the audition. It was Cathy's smile that made me decide not to climb through the window and run away. Now I wonder if it is her turn to run away. I know she doesn't like New York very much.

I race up the stairs from the subway, down the street, and around the corner to the stage door. I am late for the warm-up, but everyone is moving slowly. Nobody feels like singing tonight, and Josh knows it's because of Cathy. He cuts our warm-up session short and sends us back to our dressing rooms.

"I don't think she ever got over Mosake dumping her like that," Tisha says.

Another girl whispers, "I saw her. She was close to tears."

"If you ask me, it's all Mosake's fault," Sipho snarls. "Him and his bloody temper."

"You're all wrong, you know. She's homesick. She doesn't have what it takes to make it here in New York." Who else but Gloria would say something like that?

"But why so soon?" Nongeni protests. "It's not right. It's our fault too. None of us gave a thought to how she might be feeling.

She doesn't get the recognition we do, and we all depend on her so much. I know I've never once said thank you to her. Have any of you?''

Nobody answers that, and I feel helpless when Cathy comes through the door behind Big Joe. ''Ten minutes to curtain,'' he says.

Cathy is tense, brittle, trying hard to be cheerful. Good-byes are hard for me. There's a tiny place in my mind that would like to go with her.

''Seraki, don't look so sad,'' she says with a weak smile. ''You should be happy for me, I'm going home!''

''I'll miss you,'' is all I can think of to say when she pulls me toward her and gives me a fierce hug.

''Don't let him become too strong, Seraki,'' she whispers in my ear. ''Stand up to him. I can't anymore, but you can.'' She squeezes my arm with a strength I never knew she had.

I look at her, and then must turn away. I do not want to see her tears falling on us as she circles the room to say her good-byes.

''Cathy, stay.''

''Please don't go.''

''At least watch the show one last time.''

''We'll do it for you,'' I say, but I know that inside she has left New York already and is tasting the dust and feeling the sunshine of home.

ON THE STREETS

Today it's the first of February. Back in South Africa it's the middle of summer. Not so here. It is still winter in Manhattan, but every now and then we have a day when the sun shines and the sky is blue. But just when I think the cold might be over, another freezing, snowy day sends people back to their thick coats, scarves, woolen hats, and their winter scowls. I can't wait to be hot again, I mean really hot from the sun, not this fuzzy warmth from heaters. Arturo says that when the summer comes it can be so hot here that you wish all over again for the winters. I'm hoping to be home before the New York summer comes.

It's been two weeks since Cathy left. The city doesn't allow you to miss someone for long; holes like that get filled quickly.

We finished our recording session early today, and Sipho and I decided to visit Yankee Stadium in the Bronx. I've heard a lot about the Bronx, all bad things: "It isn't a nice part of town; people like to pretend it isn't there; you shouldn't go there; it's dangerous." It sounded a little like Soweto, so Sipho and I thought we'd check it out.

Together we go down into the stink of the subway to hop on a train. The Bronx will be easy to find. Everyone knows where it is.

"Does this train go to the Bronx?" I ask a couple of guys sitting in the subway car.

"If you want to meet your black brothers in ghetto land, you've picked the right train, man!" one of the white boys with a leather jacket says. The other two sitting with him burst out laughing.

They think they're funny. I feel Sipho grip my arm.

"Come on, Seraki, it's not worth it," he says, pulling me to the other end of the subway car. He's right. They are not worth the trouble, and as the subway car passes through each station, we are soon talking about Sipho's favorite topic—America.

"I thought America would be like it is on TV," he says enthusiastically, "like 'The Love Boat' or 'Dallas.' Back home when I was hungry or far away from my family, someone would always take me in. I wouldn't have to eat from a dustbin like you see people do here. And what I don't understand, Seraki, is that there's so much money in New York. You can see it every place! And yet there are so many poor people."

"It's just the same as back home, Sipho," I answer. "A few people get their hands on the really big bucks, while the rest just struggle. Look at that headline: 'City Boss Pockets 2.5 Mil,' " I say, as the subway car pulls up at our stop, and we get out to walk along the platform. I notice that the white guys have also gotten off the subway car and are walking behind us.

Strolling down the street, my hands deep in my pockets against the cold wind, I feel strong and independent. Here in America I can go to any neighborhood, and I can be anything I want to be. New York does that to me. It makes me feel tall like the skyscrapers. I'm part of this city now, at least in the daytime. I'm not so comfortable with the night yet. There are still too many shadows and signals I don't understand.

"Hey, guys! Where'd you get those fancy shoes, dude? You look real sharp!"

We look across the street to see if the man in a long overcoat is calling to us. He is and we keep walking until he comes across the street and blocks our way.

"You come here to make a score, eh? Take a hit?"

He's not a man, but a boy. He's tall, probably about sixteen, but he looks tough.

"No, thanks, we're just looking," I say, and then realize how stupid that sounds. The foreigners and white South Africans who ride those tour buses through Soweto are also "just looking." "What I mean is we're just walking around."

"You wanna rock? Try this stuff," he says, pulling a plastic bag of what looks like Hotel Wellington sugar cubes from his pocket. "It'll make you feel really good. You got troubles, this stuff will take care of everything. It's pure, clean junk and I'll sell it to you guys cheap."

They've got their own kind of *muti* here. Only they don't call it *muti*. In Manhattan it's called money. In the Bronx they call it crack. Either way, it's supposed to be able to make you feel good, make you strong, make the world a different place.

"No thanks—we don't want any," Sipho answers.

The boy sniggers.

"Getting yourself some new customers?" It's the smart guy from the train and his two friends, who have walked up behind us. They crowd around Sipho and me.

"Looks like we've got ourselves some real live monkeys here!" the crack dealer says over our heads.

I want to push past them. "Come on, Sipho," I say. "Let's go."

"Hey, listen to these dudes talk. They sound real wild . . ."

". . . like they've just come down out of the trees."

"Hey man," a boy with a crooked nose shouts. "What's your rush?"

Sipho's nervous—he's smiling a lot—but these New Yorkers don't frighten me. They're just street kids acting tough.

"Come on, monkey! Let's hear some more of that jungle-speak," the smart guy says. He looks older than the others, about seventeen, and is swinging a loop of silver chain that is attached to his belt.

Arturo warned me about those chains. There's a stiletto knife fastened at the other end, and these guys know how to use them—with deadly speed, Arturo said.

"You monkeys coming home?" the chain-swinger says, blocking our way.

"You come needing a banana?" Crooked-nose asks, and the others think this is very funny and start pounding him on the back and making monkey sounds.

I swear at them. It's a mistake. They all hoot, and try to mimic what I'd said.

"I told you, guys. They're straight out of the jungle!"

"More like they crawled up from the bottom of the river."

"Where do you two jungle-bunnies come from?"

That's it!

I drive my fist into Chain-swinger's stomach, and duck as his stiletto swishes past my head. Sipho shouts. Someone's grabbing at my coat. I pull away, right into a fist in my face. Somehow I stay on my feet and duck another punch aimed at my head.

I can't help Sipho. He's on his knees, but I'm too busy laying punches into Crooked-nose to help him. I catch a glimpse of the stiletto coming for me again, and sidestep as it tears into the side of my jacket. I move fast, smashing down on the hand holding the knife. The stiletto falls, but the chain keeps it from hitting the ground, and with a jerk of his wrist it's back in his hand. Chain-swinger's laughing, enjoying this.

I tuck my chin in, drive my head into his face. He falls to the ground. He's not laughing anymore. I yank at the stiletto and it comes free from his belt. Sirens scream, and red and blue lights flash across his face.

My arm is in the air to throw the knife away when a rough hand grabs my wrist and throws me to the ground. A uniform is looming over me. A cop yanks the weapon from my hand and pulls me off Chain-swinger.

"Okay! That's enough!" he hollers, and suddenly there's a crowd around us.

"Lock them up, sergeant, we don't want their filth here. They've turned this neighborhood rotten," a man with a huge belly screams in my face.

"You blacks are always causing trouble," a woman in curlers, with a pale, wrinkled face, yells down from her apartment window.

Where did they all come from? The street was empty a few minutes ago. Now people are coming in close to swear at us. Others are standing in groups on the steps of the apartments. The officers aren't paying any attention to the hecklers. They are too busy handcuffing everyone and shoving them into their cars. I notice that the crack dealer got away. The three white guys are shoved into one police car, and Sipho and I are pushed into another.

I try to tell the policeman what happened.

"You too, boy. Whatever you got to say, I'm not interested," he says, pushing me into the car.

I feel my face. My hand comes away covered with blood. Sipho moves over as I climb into the backseat. He's got the beginnings of a nasty black eye, but he shrugs and grins at me.

"Just like back home, hey, Seraki?" he says.

The police station is crowded and noisy: Two cops are yelling at a drunk, a woman is sobbing, cops are calling for release forms, and three street women are demanding their rights. At every desk officers are trying to make themselves heard over the uproar. Sipho and I are waiting on a bench for our officers to finish filling out forms.

"What time is it?" I ask him.

"Five-ten." We stare at each other. We're both thinking that we're never going to make it to the theater in time.

I try to explain again, being as polite as I can. "You don't understand, officer. Sipho and I, we've got a show tonight, and we've got to—"

"Listen, kid, I can only release you to your parents. You're both underage. Rules are rules. Besides, you were caught with a dangerous weapon, and that's an offense in this state. We got laws here, so just shut up and things might go easier for you." He turns back to shuffling and scribbling on the forms in front of him.

"Can we make a phone call?" I ask, pleading with the officer as he gets up to leave.

"One." He takes me to the pay phone and stands by me while I try to remember the theater's phone number. I look over at Sipho and he shakes his head like he can't remember it either. The only number I can remember is Nongeni's at the Block. Her number is busy, so I guess at the Hotel Wellington's number.

Arturo can't come to the phone. I can only leave a message.

"Sipho, use your call to try Nongeni again." This time the phone rang and no one answered.

The officer takes us back to the bench. "Can I try one more time?" I ask.

"Nope. That ain't allowed."

"Rules are rules!" Sipho says.

"Yup! You boys are learning fast."

"Seraki, we've got to find someone else. What if Arturo doesn't get the message?" Sipho says, looking around the crowded police station, where no one's doing much to help anyone.

137

"I'll try to phone Bob Haskins. Maybe he can . . . I'll ask that policeman over there," I say, and walk quietly over to another desk. "Excuse me, sir, can I make another phone call?"

"Sorry, son, you've made your call and that's all you're allowed. Come with me," the cop says, getting up.

So, this is what it's like being in prison: sitting in a corner, waiting. I look over at Sipho. He hasn't said anything since they locked us in here. He's scared, but he's trying not to show it. I'm scared, too, until I think of Phakane. How he would laugh if he could see me now. You had to go all the way to America to get locked up in prison, he'd say.

"Seraki, what's taking them so long?" Sipho asks for the fiftieth time.

"How should I know?" Then we don't talk again. We sit here in this long cement room with benches along the walls. They call it a waiting cell, and that's what everyone in here is doing. The men sitting across from us are staring through the bars into another cell where other men are staring back. It is quiet, smelly, and cold. Someone calls out to no one that he has to make a phone call. Nobody responds.

Sipho and I sit in our corner, trying not to attract too much attention. One man keeps coming over to us, wanting to show us something in his jacket. A black guy in the cell across the corridor yells at him to leave us alone.

"Sipho, relax. Arturo will get us out."

"But it's been almost an hour. I can't stand this waiting. What about the show tonight?"

"I know! I know! What time is it now?"

"Five past six."

"We'll never make it!"

Neither of us has mentioned Mosake—what he will say, or do, when he finds out that we've missed a show. I try to imagine if the others could do it without us. They couldn't. They would have to cancel. I wish Cathy was still here.

I feel sick.

Maybe Josh can restage some of the numbers—and maybe Mosake won't find out.

My nose hurts. It's stopped bleeding. There's dried blood on my shirt. My jacket is cut, and, checking the pricking sensation I have on my knees, I find them badly grazed.

"How's your eye feeling, Sipho?"

"It's stinging like crazy. What do I look like?"

"Not pretty. What time is it now?"

"Six-fifteen. We should be at the theater by now."

I think about the others, changing into their costumes, putting on makeup, and warming up for tonight's show. And here we are sitting in prison on the other side of town. If only I hadn't punched that guy in the stomach . . .

"Seraki! Sipho!"

It's Arturo. We both jump at the sound of his voice.

"You wanna get out of Sing Sing to sing sing tonight all you gotta do is call Arturo!"

"Arturo, you did it! I knew you would!" Sipho says.

"Come on, you jailbirds—how we gonna do the show tonight with you two locked up?" jokes Bob Haskins. He slaps Sipho on the back through the bars.

"Where's Nongeni?" I ask as a cop unlocks the cell. "Arturo, where's Nongeni?" I repeat.

"I couldn't find her, so I phoned the theater and spoke to Bob . . ."

"Arturo here, he's a whiz, I tell you boys. One in a million. And did he get us here fast?" Bob Haskins booms, as we push through the front office and out onto the street. "Come on, kids! We've got a show to put on tonight! Meet José, Arturo's cousin."

"The fastest hack in town," Arturo says, pushing us into the backseat of a taxi with a running engine.

I get into the cab and glance back at the police station.

My neck prickles: Mosake is standing on the steps, shaking a cop's hand. As he turns to leave he catches me looking at him. He flicks his head angrily. I think of the crocodile: a dangerous animal when roused.

"Seraki, I couldn't help it," Arturo whispers beside me. "I didn't know that Mosake would be in Bob's office when I rang."

Mosake's face appears at the cab window. He taps sharply at the glass. I wind the window down.

"Have you any idea what it would cost me to cancel tonight's show? A bloody fortune!" he says, glaring at Sipho and me. "You two—after the show tonight—my office!"

He slaps the roof of the taxi, and José pulls away from the curb. It's six-forty.

The curtain goes up at seven. It'll take us at least thirty minutes to get to the theater from this part of town.

We're never going to make it.

THE CROCODILE'S LAIR

Darkness. Then in a shaft of flashlight, pipes, cobwebs, a low ceiling, then darkness again. Water dripping and the low murmur of an engine humming. The shaft of light returns, blinds me. I raise my arms to protect my face. I cannot move anymore. Then darkness again and the rotting, dark, moldering smell of death. I swallow the taste of decay with gulps of stale air. I tremble, but not from this cold floor or the hard wall I am up against.

We are under the stage, below the boiler room, under the earth, in his lair. There are no windows, only blackness, the wandering beam of light, this smell, and him. Breathing comes with difficulty. I am out of air, sweating in the cold.

He's dragged us down to a black hole under the theater. He's hidden us, thrown us away. He's leaving us to rot.

We are being punished.

I won't cry.

Nobody touches me. Nobody makes me cry.

I lie where he's thrown me, my knees drawn to my chin, my face down for protection.

I will not cry.

He stands over me with his *sjambok* raised. He's breathing rapidly. I can't see his face; his flashlight is behind him, hanging from a pipe.

"I warned you boys about this, but you, Seraki, have always resisted me. I warned you!"

I try to shut out his gentle, persistent voice, but I can't. I wince away from the *sjambok*. He waits for me to relax, then he will lash out. I curl up tighter, clenching my knees, my teeth. I can smell his sweat, his anticipation.

He lowers the *sjambok* and moves away. The light goes out. A loud clang echoes through the cellar. I flinch, waiting for the pain.

Sipho whimpers somewhere in the darkness. Was it five minutes or an hour ago that I stopped telling him it's going to be okay?

Out of the darkness he speaks again. "The show went up late tonight. It was almost canceled. That must never, never happen again." He pauses. His breathing is quieter. "You have broken the most important rule in theater. You both need to learn a lesson."

He opens the heavy door of the cellar, and green neon floods briefly into the room. Standing in the doorway, he places the crocodile on top of one of the machines.

"The crocodile will watch over you tonight," he says.

He closes the door with a dull, permanent thud and we are once again in the dark. I hear him mounting the metal staircase, and then there's silence.

Something scurries to the left of me.

"Seraki! Is that you?" Sipho wails.

"No! I thought it was you."

Something runs over my foot. I yell, kick out, jump up, bang my head against something hard.

"Ouch!"

"Seraki?"

"It's all right, Sipho! I'm okay. I just banged my head." I reach up to my head and beyond to find the ceiling. I cringe and quickly wipe the cobwebs from my head. "I think it was a rat," I say, sweating, and trying to steady the banging in my chest.

The smell is stronger now. Holding my hand to my nose doesn't help. My hand smells of rotting too.

"Seraki, where are you?"

"I'm here. He's gone," I say, speaking loud to comfort myself. "You okay?"

"I'm so cold."

"But are you okay? Can you see me?"

"No, I'm hurt. I fell . . . ," he stammers. "And I'm scared . . ." I search for him, stumble toward his gulps of air, the low sound of his crying.

My hands carve out the shapes of the machines. I pass small buttons of light—red, green, yellow—but there is not enough light to find Sipho. Gauges quiver. Tisha would know what these are. My guess is air-conditioning machines, heating, and maybe the hydraulics for moving the stage. There must be a ventilator shaft in here, and a light. I must find the light. I stumble as Sipho pulls me down to where he is crouched.

"Why, Seraki? Why this bad?"

"Shhhh, shhhh," is all I can say, and hold him.

We sit like that, trying to share the warmth we can give each other. Soon we are both shivering.

Water drips in the darkness. The steady murmur of the engine starts up again. Shapes begin to emerge out of the blackness. I must figure out where the door is. The light switch must be by the door.

Mosake has left us here. He won't be coming back. We must make ourselves more comfortable. "What time is it, Sipho?" My voice surprises me. It sounds stronger than I feel.

Sipho squirms out of my arms. "My watch is broken."

"Come on, let's start feeling along the walls. There are pipes. Maybe some of them are warm." Maybe I can find the light.

"Don't leave me, Seraki. Stay close."

"Come on, we'll look together. Hold on to my shirt."

Stiffly, we untangle ourselves and search along the walls, our hands outstretched, feeling blindly for warmth. I fear touching the rotting thing, but I don't tell Sipho this. It must be very near. The smell is so bad, my eyes are tearing.

"Here!" Sipho calls out.

He has found two lukewarm pipes running upward past what feels like a shelf of cement, long enough for both of us to sit on. "Stay right here," I say, and follow the wall to where I think the door must be. There is no light switch. I feel past more cobwebs to a light bulb, inside a wire cage over my head. The switch must be outside the door.

I stumble back to Sipho.

"I found these," he says, and directs my hand to newspapers and a coarse sack. He has laid them on the ledge. We squeeze in next to each other, and wrap our legs and arms around the pipes. I rest my cheek against this warmth which somehow connects us to the world outside.

I wake up in the darkness, thirsty. Hungry too. Sipho has fallen over and lies half in my lap. The pipes are icy cold. I cannot feel my legs. I move and thousands of prickings tell me they are still there, hanging toward the floor.

It is as dark as it was when we fell asleep. I don't know how long I slept. It feels like only an hour. I don't wake Sipho. I must stay still and think.

Last night we arrived at the theater at five past seven. José drove like a madman and Arturo was right—he is the fastest taxi driver in the world.

The other kids were full of questions, but there was no time to answer them. Sipho's eye was swollen shut. Not even makeup could help that, and there was no time to put any on, either. Big Joe went to the front of the house to delay the final bell until Tisha gave him clearance. Nongeni helped us into our costumes. She was great. She didn't ask any questions.

I punched the air with my swollen fist at twenty-five minutes past seven. I don't think the audience cared what time we started. They saw the whole show, though it wasn't one of our best, but they saw everything they paid to see and at the end they clapped like they always do.

After the show Bob Haskins sent the other kids home. Sipho and I went to Mosake's office. We had never been up there before. We wandered through the carpeted corridors, past the heavy, polished wooden doors. I kept telling Sipho that everything would be all right. We made it. The show happened. He can't be too angry, I said. He got his performance.

When we entered the office he didn't look at us. He picked up the crocodile from his desk, stuffed it into his pocket, and motioned for us to follow him. He took us down the elevator, across the marbled foyer, and back through the empty, quiet theater. Trying to keep up with his long strides, I could see that he was angry. Why hadn't he said anything? Usually he explodes into a rage that leaves you deaf.

We followed him across the stage—I remember looking around hoping to see Big Joe. Then we walked down the stairs and under the stage. That was when I started shaking. Why was he taking us so deep under the theater?

"Where are we going?" I asked.

He turned around and from under his jacket he took out the *sjambok*. "Just follow me, or I will use this," he said.

We walked through tunnels, past prop rooms and stage sets from other shows. Then down more steps to the bottom of the theater, and down a spiral staircase, past the stage machinery, past the power room and then down a ladder, to another narrower corridor ending at a neon light and a large metal door. That was when Mosake took out his flashlight and that was when I knew it was going to be bad.

By the thin green light I saw how frightened Sipho was. I wanted to whisper to him not to let Mosake know, but I was scared too.

He ordered us to open the door. It was stiff and heavy.

Mosake squeezed his hand around the back of my neck and threw me into the black hole. I stumbled in the dark and fell. When

I turned back to the green light, I saw Sipho, too, falling hard against something in the dark room.

Mosake pulled the door closed behind him, and the lashing of the *sjambok* began. We scrambled blindly around the small space, trying to hide from the swishing tail of the leather whip. Then his flashlight found us and we stopped moving. Exhausted we sat, crouched, waiting for the blows. None came.

He left us with uncertainty. He left us with the memory of his flailing *sjambok*.

Sipho stirs, and, springing up, he thrashes around. He screams. I hold him down. We wrestle. I shout his name. I try to stop him from bumping against the metal pipes.

"Sipho! Hey, Sipho!"

He stops thrashing around and calms down. I feel his body shaking.

"I had a terrible dream," he says, breathing hard, "and when I woke up I was still in the nightmare."

"No, your dream is over. Listen. It must be daytime. The night is finished. Listen . . ."

From far away we can hear soft music. Somewhere a radio is playing. We hold our breaths to listen to that sweet sound of life trickling down to us. And then from even farther away, the thick hush of traffic filters through the cracks to our dark hole. The building shakes. A subway is passing us deep underground. We sit still, listening to all those bright signs of day. A police siren wails. Down here that too is comforting.

"What time do you think it is?" Sipho asks.

"I don't know. Maybe early morning by the sound of that traffic."

"Do you think we should try and get out of this room?"

"Let's see if there's another way out," I say, gingerly getting up and feeling my body ache all over. It's hard to stretch in the small space.

"Seraki, don't go away."

"I won't, trust me, I won't."

I fumble around the small room again. There is only the one door we came through. There are no windows, no ventilator shafts, no trapdoor, no escaping from the room. Nothing has changed but the stench. It is worse than sour milk, worse than moldy fruit, worse even than the stink of sick and urine behind Auntie Somoza's. The smell eats at my nostrils, bites at my throat.

I return to our sleeping place, collapse next to our pipes. They are warm again, and we curl ourselves around them, to wait.

"We have a show tonight. He must come soon," I say, wondering how long Mosake plans to keep us here.

We talk about our families, about home. Sipho tells me of his father, who works at the mines. How rarely he sees his father, how much older he seems every time he comes home from the mines. He talks of his mother, who has lovers behind his father's back.

I tell him about Phakane, how King Danny threatened my family with the ax, how I got to see my brother in prison. As I talk it sounds like a story I am making up from long ago. It's hard to think that I still have a brother called Phakane and that he is still alive.

We are waiting, hungry and thirsty.

Sipho is crying again, softly. He is not ashamed of the tears that must be falling from his cheeks. I have no more words to comfort him. He talks of dark things: how his father locked him up in a suitcase as a child, how his mother locked him away when her boyfriends came to visit. I don't want to hear anymore, but I can't tell him to stop talking, and he doesn't until his voice gets slow and tired and I think he has fallen asleep.

I am waiting, stiff, and hurting for something to drink.

I wonder if the others are worried about us. If there is anything they can do. I know Arturo cannot help. He wouldn't be able to do anything for us this time. But what about Teddy? By now he must know we are not at the Block. What has Teddy said to the others? What has Mosake told them all?

I fly over Soweto, sweeping low over the shanties, shebeens, taxi stands, train stations, and factories until I sail above the busy

Golden Highway, and then, veering away from the double black stripe, I zoom over the banks and down the slopes of the veld, the tall veld grass whizzing past beneath me, and fly into the country of my grandfather.

My flying becomes slower, more like gliding, as I spiral above the deep brown river that runs next to my family's kraal. There are no people in the kraal, but gliding above the brown line of water that winds through the country, I spot, far below, on the riverbank, a crocodile sunning itself on the white sand.

I float gently down to the water's edge until I am only a hand's touch away from the monster. It is asleep. Its eyes are closed. Always I want to get closer. As I step nearer, the crocodile yawns, and past the jagged rows of teeth, deep inside its stomach, I see my father, Phakane, Uncle, Ma, and Sweets.

I have no choice but to reach into its mouth and try to find my father's hand. The crocodile is still yawning, and while I am searching for my father's hand, one of its scaly, hooded eyes opens. We stare at each other. I don't have much time.

I reach desperately for a hand, clawing for something that feels human, and then pull, pull, and try to jump into the air to fly away, but the jumping doesn't help. I remain solidly on the ground.

The crocodile is awake. Its tail flicks from side to side, its red eyes glisten. I try to run away, but the hand I hold drags me back. I can't seem to move fast enough. I pull the bodies out of the crocodile, but they are heavy, and I can take only one step at a time. I cry, "Hold on to each other. Don't let go!"

But the crocodile swallows all those I've pulled out, steadily eating its way toward me. But I won't be eaten and so, dragging the people, I run, run, downhill to the gorge at the bottom of the hill, until I fall over the drop and soar once again into the sky, pulling all the people I care about behind me.

In the sky we all hold hands and make a long people-chain: Phakane, Ma, Uncle, Father, and I. Sipho is with us, too, and I think that is Nongeni at the end beside Sweets. I let go of my father's hand and we race through the sky. The flapping of our clothes, the noise in our ears, the wind flattening our faces. Tears are streaming down my cheeks.

I am dreaming of tiny lights in dark places. I am chasing the glowing pin pricks, but I stumble over hidden objects, skin my knees, graze the palms of my hands. I get up and chase after the flickering, which slowly grows into a rectangle of green light.

The metal door is open. I blink at the shape of a man.

He is standing in the doorway. The beam of his flashlight searches us out. I don't want to stand up, I don't want the ray of light to fall on me. It does.

"Seraki? Sipho? Come, I have brought you some food, and something hot to drink. You must be very tired."

Sipho squints. "Who is that?"

"Come, Sipho, you are hungry. Here, let me help you down." His voice is gentle, sympathetic.

He comes over to us and helps me lift Sipho out of my lap. I half close my eyes to the bright light.

"I'm sorry, Mosake, I'm so sorry. I'll never do it again," Sipho cries out, holding onto Mosake, as the man lifts him up and takes him into the light.

"Come, Seraki. It's over now." He speaks like he is our savior, our father. Despite my anger, I am grateful to him for letting me out. I also want to collapse into his arms, the way Sipho does, but I cannot let him touch me. I can no longer trust this man who is cruel one moment and so kind the next.

We are led out of the room. My eyes adjust to the light and I see, up in one of the corners of the room, the shape of a swollen dead cat, caught in the blades of a ventilation fan. A rat scurries along the pipes away from the open stomach of the dead animal. The juices of my stomach rise to my throat, but I have nothing inside me to be sick with. I must stop and retch just outside the heavy metal door and lean my head against the wall, above the light switch.

We climb the stairs back to the stage and are taken to one of the empty dressing rooms. Water, food, and coffee are laid out on the table. Mosake sits on one of the beds, watching as we approach the food. Sipho bites hungrily into a hamburger. I stare at the man who locked us away.

"Come, Seraki. Eat. You know why I had to do what I did," he says, almost whispering. "And it won't happen again, will it?"

"No, Mosake. Never," Sipho says, his mouth full of burger.

"Seraki?"

I nod, not taking my eyes off his.

"The others mustn't know about this. If you tell them I will send you home, without any money. Do you understand?"

I pour myself some coffee and glance at Sipho. There is panic in his eyes. He doesn't want to be sent home. I look back at Mosake and nod. He cannot send me home. He will not have my money.

"Good. If anyone asks, you spent the night with me in my apartment. We had a long talk. You've learned your lesson and now we understand each other."

He rises to leave, but pauses by the door. "Now you must both take a shower, and then sleep. Here. You have three hours before the others arrive for tonight's show. By then you must be as fresh as they are."

You are right, I think, you have taught me too well. Now I know everything about the crocodile. I have survived its lair, and you, Producer Number One, have made a mistake of your own.

In the shower, with the hot water running over my bruises, I think of Phakane. Of how he said that being on the inside made men stronger. I am stronger. Now I am still inside, and as I lie down in the light and warmth of the room, I look over at Sipho sleeping on the other bed. He is my brother now, too.

I will not sleep. I will lie here awake. Thinking. Plotting.

THE UNDERBELLY

When I was a small boy, my father used to take me by train to visit his parents in the country. My grandfather knew nothing about cities—he'd never been near one—but he knew everything about the world in which he and his fathers had always lived. Grandfather's home was near a river, and so he knew a lot about crocodiles. He told me they are greatly respected because they are powerful and pitiless and cunning.

He said that often—how cunning they are.

It's a crisp, quiet Sunday morning and the city is sleeping off its usual Saturday night party. It's the only day of the week when the streets are almost empty, when walking down the pavement isn't a jostling, bumpy experience.

I am out of the Block early this morning before any of the others wake up. Even deep in the city the morning still smells fresh with sunshine and rain.

I don't want to ride the subway anywhere today, not even to the aquarium. Today I want to be out in the air. I don't want to see drunks asleep with newspapers over their faces. Yesterday I saw a headline that said: "H$_2$O Main Bursts, Thousands Flee." I would have liked to have been there for that, but since our troubles with the police, we are not supposed to go anywhere.

Every day we have to check in with Linda at four o'clock by phone and we have to be at the theater a whole hour earlier than we used to. Mosake's become crazy that one of us will be late for a performance. Linda told Nongeni it's because he had to pay overtime to all the backstage crew at the theater, the orchestra, and even the front-of-house staff. That's what the union rules are in New York, she said: If a show finishes late, you pay.

We are no longer allowed out on the streets alone. No one is supposed to go out after a performance. Except Gloria, who Mosake said was responsible. She goes out almost every night with her American boyfriend. Finally she's got herself one with a car.

Mosake says we've been allowed too much freedom, too much time to get into mischief. Keep them off the streets, he's commanded Josh.

I don't care if Mosake finds out about my basketball on Sundays. I'm not afraid of him anymore.

Even though it's early, the guys from school will already be warming up for our Sunday morning basketball.

I wish Sipho were walking along the river with me to the game. He used to like playing basketball. Now he doesn't want to go anywhere or do anything. I think he's the only one who's obeying Mosake's orders. He doesn't want to share a room with me anymore, and he's changed places with Teddy. He won't talk to me either. Not since that night. It lies between us like a sleeping brown snake, hidden by the dust of the veld.

We both know it's there even though we can't see it. It's as though we'll be bitten if we talk about it. He acts tense and embarrassed around me, and if I catch his eye, he quickly looks away. I think he is ashamed; he wants to pretend that it never happened. I wish he would talk to me. I wish I could make him understand there's nothing wrong with being afraid: It's only stupid people who are never frightened.

I start jogging lightly and look out at the stuff floating in the Hudson River.

My grandfather once told me that you can never see a crocodile in the river because it looks like a log.

"And that's the danger," he told me, his voice low and solemn. "Once he has you, he holds you under the water until you drown, and then he drags you into the depths of the river, and stores you away in some underwater hole in the bank until you rot. Only then does he feed.''

"Can you ever overcome him?" I asked.

"Yes," my grandfather answered, "but never go for his back. There he's tougher than an elephant. Stay away from his mouth too. There's rotting flesh caught between his teeth and it's poisonous. A scratch from those teeth will kill you. Also watch out for his tail—with one flick he can break a man's leg. If you want to get him, the way is through his underbelly. Why do you think he sits so tight to the ground?" My grandfather chuckled. "He protects himself where he knows he is weak. So go for his underbelly. There his skin is soft, and a knife can easily find his heart. Go for his underbelly!''

My grandfather is dead now, and I didn't remember everything he told me until the other day. I was in Mr. Kleinholtz's bookshop when he showed me a new coffee-table book all about the wild animals of Africa. My grandfather was right: That book also said if you want to get a crocodile, you must strike at the underbelly.

I jog up to the court. The guys have started without me, but I am greeted by a basketball thrown hard and fast to my chest. I catch it, run, dribbling past two players, spin around someone else, and jump into the air. I loft the ball and watch as it kisses the rim and drops neatly through the net. *Swish.*

"Ouch! The Broadway Star is hot this morning!" one of the boys shouts, and runs toward me for a high five. We jump, slapping our hands together.

He's right. I am hot this morning.

I've been thinking a lot about my grandfather's advice.

We've finished five fast games of half-court and I surprised myself with how many points I scored for my side. This is the first time my side's not buying the burgers for the winners.

"Tough luck, Zeke," one of my teammates says to the captain of the losers' side. We are sitting close together at a bright orange booth in McDonald's.

"You got us today, boys! And I was sure that our song-and-dance-man'd be slipping his bucks to old Micky D. today. Now

I'm busted for the week. How much you make down there on the Great White Way, anyhow?"

"One hundred and fifty a week."

Some of the guys whistle loudly at that, but Zeke says, "Don't sound right to me. You sure nobody's ripping you off?"

"We're a big cast," I answer, "and we don't have to pay anything for rent."

"Maybe, but it doesn't sound right." He changes the subject to the kind of money the pro–basketball players make. They're talking millions, which sounds unbelievable to me. But what do I know?

Basketball Sunday is over. It's not time yet for *iSezela*'s Monday. I'm sitting alone in my room. In the other room Sipho and Teddy are watching basketball on TV. I've got more important things to do. All that talk about money over lunch has started me thinking about us.

Exactly how rich is our show making us kids, I wonder? I think I make a lot of money, but how much, exactly? Thousands of people come to see the show each week. I wonder how much it all adds up to. I take out a piece of my writing paper to do the sums.

Bob Haskins says the Liberty Globe seats twelve hundred people. An average ticket is sixty dollars.

I can hardly grasp the number that jumps off the page at me. That's seventy-two thousand dollars—a night! And we've had full houses every night since we opened. Times nine shows a week . . .

The zeros dazzle me. The box office take is somewhere near six hundred and forty thousand dollars. That's over half a million dollars—a week! And we've been performing for how many weeks? I don't even know anymore. And all I get is one hundred and fifty dollars?

I'm so grateful! Thank you, *Baas!* Thank you, *Baas!*—holding out my hands and clapping them together. I can't believe it! We must have made millions of dollars by now. So what if Mosake had to pay out overtime and our rent?

I've found the underbelly.

Now I must find my weapon!

It's Monday night, and we've just finished another show. We are pushing through the crowds, like we always do, to get on the subway. Ever since I did that figuring of the money, I can't help thinking our show is like an expensive takeout. The people come in, grab a Maci*Sezela,* and swallow it whole. Then they burp, and return to their routines. We are forgotten like the empty wrappers in the trash bin. And we're not worth much more than that either.

I don't want to think like this, but I can't help it. Doing the show has become like working in a sausage factory. We just stuff and roll them out, performance after performance. It's taking all my energy to be "up" all the time.

I was glad when our recording sessions finished, but I'm sorry that I've had to quit school. I'm just too tired to go anymore. I have to save everything I have for my fast-food-with-no-aftertaste performances. And I hate myself for sounding like Uncle does when he's had too much to drink. That's when he starts feeling sorry for himself.

We pass the theater where *A Chorus Line* is playing. They've been at it for years! Then past Dunkin' Donuts: forty-six varieties; past the topless women on movie marquees, past that rotten watch seller who said he'd never seen me or my watch before. Sipho and Teddy are way ahead of me now. Tisha and a couple of the boys in front of me are blending in with the New York crowd. It's their leather jackets and the girls' pink high tops and bobby socks that make them look so much like everyone else. All the boys have their caps tilted at the fashionable angle, and all the girls, even Nongeni, are wearing floppy earrings and their hair in braids, just like Linda's. Only Gloria is clicking along in high heel shoes, her long, tight dress trailing on the dirty street. She's getting to look more and more like Mosake's Diamond Lady. I wonder why she's going back to the Block with us at all. Maybe she got dumped by her American boyfriend.

"Don't you just love looking at all the people on the streets at night, Seraki? Hey, Seraki?" Nongeni says, touching my hand.

"Sorry. Yes, sometimes."

I wish I were by myself tonight. I don't want to have anything to do with the show. I don't even want to be in New York.

I want to walk under the yellow moons in Soweto, stand in the shadow of Mrs. Mcebi's house, watch my father clean the primus stove, and then go inside our shack to eat my mother's cooking.

I suppose this pain is from the letter I got today, from my father, the first he has ever written to me. It was short and filled with spelling mistakes, but it was obvious that he had taken a long time to write those few lines. He told me about the new house they are moving into. It is made of brick and has lights and water. He told me about his job as caretaker for the Community Center, and about a police raid at Auntie Somoza's. At the end he thanked me for the money I had sent them. And he said that he was proud of me. It's a good thing I was alone when I read it. It made me cry.

Across the street there's a man standing on a box, preaching at the passersby. He's holding a placard: "The World Is Doomed!"

I'm feeling pretty doomed myself.

Nobody ever seems to pay any attention to these preachers. Everyone's too busy, like in our song, too busy to think about the future. They head for the subway, buy hot dogs, sell street goods, scoop up the news from the newsstands. Even the newspapers only talk about what's already past. Never about the future. That headline over there on the late edition: "Rev Caught with Pants Down." I wonder what that's all about?

"What did you think of tonight's performance?" Nongeni asks, interrupting my thoughts, as we go down to the subway platform, to wait for our earthworm.

"What?"

"Tonight's performance. It was awful," she says.

"Probably our worst ever," I say, impatiently pushing my way through a gang of street kids jiving onto the train car, their boom box blasting.

"Something's wrong, something's changed," Nongeni says, having to shout over their clamor, the noise of the doors closing, the train rattling down the dark tunnel. "On stage tonight, we did everything we've always done, but there was no sparkle."

155

She's right. Tonight I felt like a machine, making all the right moves, saying all the right words, singing the right notes, but I wasn't really there. When I ran out onto the stage for my first entrance, and shouted, my fist raised to the sky, it felt like nothing . . .

"What's wrong with us?"

"We're dead."

For a second everyone on the stage stared at me and tried to cover up for whatever it was that I did wrong. It felt terrible, like performing in an enormous, empty white room that was soaking up all of me.

"What's wrong with Sipho?" she asks.

"I don't know," I answer, except I do. He's become heavy and slow. He's lost his shine, and his jokes don't get the laughs they used to. "I think Josh told him to cut some of his lines."

"It's like he's trying desperately not to let the show down, but the harder he tries, the worse he gets."

I look at Nongeni's reflection in the darkened glass of the subway window. I can see how upset she is. She still loves this show, even though we've done hundreds of performances.

"But it's so strange that the audience doesn't seem to notice," she says. "We got the same applause, the same cheers, the same standing ovation. Couldn't they sense something was terribly wrong?"

"And what about Mosake bouncing backstage like that to congratulate us on our 'marvelous' show?" I say, laughing.

After the final curtain fell, we left the stage without looking at one another. We were afraid of the truth. We'd just sold a lie to another audience, who had left the theater happily satisfied. They bought our lie, without even knowing it.

"He was like we'd just won him the Tony award," she says. "After tonight's performance I can't believe they've extended our run."

"Get ready, gal. Our stop is next," is all I can say. As we push our way off the train and climb the stairs I shiver, and it's not from the cold blast of night air.

Tonight, after the show, Mosake made his announcement: "The show's to be extended for another six months." He called that wonderful news. Then he came straight over to Sipho and me. He hugged us both, saying how much he'd enjoyed our performance. Sipho-Smiler just looked at him, pulled out of his arms, and left the room, trembling. I shrugged Mosake's hand off my shoulder. Nobody touches me.

But he didn't seem to notice that, or how we stared at him without saying a word.

"Isn't that great?" he shouted. "Do you understand what I said? We get to extend the show for another six months. You'll all have two weeks off and then we'll open again. The bookings for the extension are going well: The first week's already sold out. *iSezela* is still the talk of the town . . . ," he rattled on.

"Can we go home first?" Tisha blurted out, and I noticed how everyone paused in packing away their stuff to listen carefully for Mosake's reply.

"Oh, no!" He laughed. "There's no time for that! It's too far, and too expensive. Besides, I want to add a couple of new songs, and change some of the dance routines. We've got to keep the show fresh. Once you're at the top of the pile in New York, you have to work twice as hard to stay there. Anyway, why would you want to go home when you're having such a wonderful time here?"

"Because it's our home and we're tired," I mumbled, not thinking he'd hear me.

He did.

"What was that?" he asked, coming over to me.

He was grinning, but I saw the danger in his eyes. I was not going to turn away from him, so I held his gaze while I continued to pack my bag.

"What did you say, Seraki?" he asked, louder.

I stopped packing, put my bag on the floor, moved my chair under the dressing table, and switched off the lights to my mirror. Only then did I answer. By then the room had gone completely silent.

"I said the reason we want to go back to South Africa is because it is our home, and because we are tired."

"Oh!" He laughed with a forced and ugly sound. "Are you telling me that you're homesick for your shanty hovel, for your miserable life in Soweto?" He was no longer smiling. "Here, you are someone. Back there you're nothing but one of a million boys roaming the streets and trying to survive. Don't make me laugh!"

He turned to the others. They looked away, pretending to be busy, with nothing left to do. He went on, more threateningly. "There are thousands of kids back home who would kill for the chance to be doing what you're doing here. I could replace you like that," and he clicked his thumb and finger together. "Which one of you wants to go home? Come on, tell me, now's your chance. Tomorrow I'll put you on the next flight home," he said, challenging us.

Everyone looked helpless. I saw Nongeni dig deeply into her bag, not daring to meet Mosake's gaze when it rested on her.

I knew he was bluffing. He couldn't replace us that easily, but I couldn't afford to take the chance. Nobody moved or said anything. We had let him win again.

"The problem with you lot is you don't know how lucky you are. You've been given the privilege of serving iSezela . . . and don't you ever forget it."

With that, he left the dressing room.

"Seraki, I wish you'd just shut up!" Gloria hissed at me. "You're making trouble for everybody. None of us wants to go home." She looked about the room for the others' support. Everyone was gone.

I caught up with Nongeni outside the theater. She was crying.

"What's the matter, Nongeni?" I asked, putting my arm around her.

"I'm sorry, Seraki. I should have said something to help you. I don't know why I didn't say anything."

"Because you were frightened of being fired from the show, and so was I. It's okay, Nongeni, we'll find our moment."

"I love this show, you know that . . . but I would like to go

158

home for just a week, or maybe even a month. He made it sound so impossible . . ."

"Yes, I'd like to go home, too, but there's no use thinking about it," I said, hoisting my bag onto my shoulder, and wishing I had called Mosake's bluff.

Despite the brightness of the streetlights, there are shadows everywhere. Even so close to our Block, the New York night creatures come out onto the streets to sell their "hot" property, loose women, and drugs. They wear heavy, dark coats and hide their faces behind scarves and under hats. They whisper from dark alleys as we pass,

"Anything you want, I got."

A police siren wails in the cold night. There's a gunshot, or maybe it was just a car backfiring. The street people stand shivering over sidewalk gratings, and below, in the subway, a train thunders past.

Nongeni takes hold of my arm. She pulls me into a shop entrance where no one is sleeping.

"Seraki, I know Mosake did something terrible to you the night you and Sipho were late. And I understand why you don't want to tell me about it, but don't you see that what he did to you two has affected the whole cast? Something's gone wrong somewhere. Everything has become sour. Since that night, your performance has become stiff. It's almost as if you and Sipho aren't here anymore."

"I do everything I've always done before," I say.

"That's just the point. You're just doing it. There's no fire. I know you don't like hearing this, but you know it's true. And you're not the only one. The whole atmosphere has changed and the show is suffering. The trouble is I don't think anyone but me really cares anymore. And now the thought of another six months. I don't know if I can take it, Seraki," and she is crying again.

A drunken woman lurches out into the traffic, her bottle smashing on the sidewalk behind her. A yellow cab brakes sharply and its driver leans out yelling curses. She weaves back to flop down on the curb in front of us. We walk on, ignoring her.

* * *

Later in the evening Sipho's mother phones from South Africa. His father's been killed in a mining accident.

He is crying when he tells us.

"She wants me to come home for the funeral. I'm the eldest son. I should be there. She needs me."

"When will you go?" Tisha asks.

"I'll have to ask Mosake," he sobs.

No one says anything. I know what's coming.

"Use our phone, Sipho. It'll be quieter in our apartment," Tisha says.

Sipho comes back, looking terrible.

"Mosake just said, 'What about the show? Not even for a week. We have no understudies.' He said all the parts in the show are important and nobody can be spared for even one performance. I hate him and his damn show!" Sipho mumbles. And then realizing what he has said, he looks sheepishly away. "What I mean is . . . It's not you guys . . ." He stops and moves away to stand next to the window, alone.

We look at him. We look at one another.

Tisha is the first to say out loud what we are all thinking.

"I don't understand. Not after what he said last night. He said anyone who wanted to could go home, on the next flight," and she looks at each of us for an answer.

"He was bluffing," I say. "He knew no one would challenge him."

Sipho turns from the window, picks up his jacket, and leaves.

"Go with him, Seraki. You're his best friend," Nongeni cries.

"I think he wants to be alone," is all I can say.

It's taken two weeks for Sipho's mother's videocassette to arrive. He wants us all to watch it with him.

I look past the people dressed in black around the hole in the earth that is now Sipho's father's grave. I catch glimpses of Soweto, the African veld, and the wide blue sky of home.

160

THE NEWER WORLD

It's Sunday morning and I'm disobeying all of Mosake's rules at once. I left the Block without waking anyone to tell them where I was going. I didn't leave any note. I'm tired of being treated like a little kid who can't look after myself. At home I can go anywhere I want to and this morning I want to go to Mr. Kleinholtz's bookstore.

I like the way books help to get my mind away from what is in my head and into someone else's. I'm good at reading English now, and lately I've been reading westerns and spy stories. Anything that's fast and exciting and a good escape.

Mr. Kleinholtz is not here this morning, so I ask the woman at the counter if I can leave my jacket with her while I browse. "Yes, of course, you're the only one here," she says, putting my jacket away.

I am at the back of the store, in the mystery section, when I overhear a man who must have just walked in talking to the woman who rings up the sales. I am caught by the excitement in his voice. He's an African-American, smartly dressed in a slick overcoat, and tall enough to be a basketball player. From the way he's talking he's probably a businessman.

"Clarissa, I can't tell you what this means to me. I was a student at Harvard when they imprisoned him, and now, to see him walking down that dusty street, a free man . . ." He stops talking and shakes his head.

"When did it happen?" she asks. She has left the counter and is standing in the aisle.

"Moments ago! It's history, Clarissa, it's already history. I never

161

thought he'd come out alive. The world has never had such a famous prisoner."

What are they talking about?

"After this, I tell you, nothing can ever be the same in that country again."

I move closer.

"Now he's on his way to Cape Town, to deliver a speech. Will you give me the book Mr. Kleinholtz left me? I've got to get back home. I don't want to miss what's happening in Cape Town."

Cape Town?

"I'm from South Africa," I say. "What's happened?"

"You haven't heard?"

"What?"

"Nelson Mandela is a free man! He's just walked out of prison. They're breaking into every television program with news flashes from South Africa. Get yourself to a television, son. You're missing out on history. Soon, they'll be broadcasting his speech live from Cape Town."

"People all over the world will hear him," Clarissa says. "Enough of this music. I'm putting the office TV right up front here to see it," and she races to the back of the shop. "No way am I gonna miss this!"

The man laughs at me as I stare at him with my mouth hanging open.

"I had the same reaction. It's incredible, isn't it?"

"Amandla!" I shout at the top of my voice. I don't care what anybody thinks of me yelling. This is the best news I've heard. Ever!

The man lifts his hand in the air, and we do a high five.

"I've got to go." Snatching my jacket from behind the counter, I shout, "Thank you."

I've got to tell the others. They have to see this. If only we were home in Soweto.

When I get to the Block, I kick on everyone's doors. "Wake up! Wake up! Everybody, wake up!" I shout down the passageway.

"Turn on your TVs. Don't be caught sleeping when history's being made!"

"Seraki, what are you doing? It's so early." It's Nongeni, standing bleary-eyed in her T-shirt.

"You want me to let you sleep while the greatest thing in the world is happening?" I shout back to her. "Mandela is free!"

"Shooooooee!" she whistles, and then rushes back into her room shouting for the others to wake up.

I dash up the steps, burst into our apartment, and throw back the heavy drapes. Sipho groans on the sofa; Teddy leans against the doorway.

"What's going on?" he asks.

I switch on the television.

At once, we are back in South Africa. Pictures of Cape Town, Victor Verster prison, and an enormous crowd of waving, *toyi-toy*ing, hooting, hollering people are dancing on the screen. A newscaster's voice is over it all:

"Here, in South Africa, it is a day of triumph. Nelson Mandela strolled out of prison at four-fourteen P.M. local time, and greeted the waiting crowd with a dignified salute. Thus has ended twenty-seven years of imprisonment, and signals victory in the longest, most famous campaign for the release of a political prisoner in this country, or anywhere else in the world."

Teddy and Sipho are close around the television. Nongeni, Gloria, and Tisha race into our apartment, with the rest of the cast behind them. All eighteen of us squeeze in tight around the television. Everyone is talking at once.

"Shhh!"

"Turn it up, Teddy!"

"Freedom in our time, guys. Freedom in our time," Sipho yells.

"Shhh! Let's hear what he says . . . ," I shout.

"This man is going to get me there!" Tisha shouts.

"Get me there!" we all shout.

Above their noise I catch more words from the newscaster.

". . . and with Mandela's release the government has confirmed

163

that negotiations have begun for the release of hundreds of other detainees. It seems that for the first time, in this strife-ridden land, there is a moment of hope, a moment of sunshine . . .''

Phakane! An image of my brother in his blue prison uniform flashes across my mind. I am back in that gray room, looking up at my brother and watching the sparkle dance in the blackness of his eyes. I remember the last words he said to me. "I will be home soon. I promise you. We are strong inside here. Sometimes I think stronger than when we are outside."

What if he is freed? And I am stuck here, unable to celebrate with him?

"Seraki?"

I turn away from the television screen.

Nongeni is staring at me with tears in her eyes.

"Seraki? Do you think it's possible?"

"Anything is possible now," I say. "Nothing can be the same after today."

While the others *toyi-toyi* around the room, out the door, and down the passageway, I stand at my bedroom window, looking out at the block of apartments across the way. The Lady of the Plants is poking at her dying ferns, and Samson is pumping iron in the flat above her. Someone is sweeping in the empty purple apartment. On the street below people walk and walk and walk to the places they always go. Out there, nothing has changed.

In South Africa much more is happening. People there are building a new tomorrow. America may be the New World, but South Africa is a newer world. People are fighting the evils that surround them, trying to build something beautiful, something unique. A new world has started there today, and I am here.

My world has not changed. I wake up in the mornings, fill my days with useless business, sing and dance for money at night, sleep, and begin it all again. I will do another show tonight, tomorrow night, next week, and maybe all the nights for six more months. What am I building?

I envy those people on the television. All over South Africa they are singing and dancing not for money but for joy. They have beaten a crocodile.

I think about prison, about Mandela locked away since before I was born. I think about Phakane, locked away since before I began singing and dancing. They have been kept in the dark because they represented something to be feared.

And I remember my long night locked away beneath the theater. What do I represent? Arturo once asked me how it was that I was not in prison like Phakane. I am in a prison, though, only it's a different kind. I chose to work for Mosake, I chose to come to New York and become part of the cast that live like prisoners. But I am still strong—"We are strong inside." I have beaten one crocodile; now I must defeat the ones that hide in the dark inside myself.

Here, I can buy a television set, a stereo, and smart clothes, even a red sports car. I can take the ferry to Staten Island and walk down 42nd Street, but none of it seems real. Here, we live in brightly colored bubbles, but back home, in Soweto, that's where my real life is going on. After today, maybe it will be different.

Maybe the Naughty Boys will not roam the streets, and my father will not have to buy more *muti* to protect his new home. Auntie may be able to laugh at the police without fearing them. Once, when I found the skinned cat, I thought it might feel good to be naked, skinned, and dead, away from all the troubles. Let other people live with pain. Let other people fight the battles. But now I see, in the sparkle of Mandela's eyes, that that's what makes life real. He has done it. He has lived through the fights and the pain, and still he smiles.

I want to go home.

"Seraki, why don't you phone your parents?" Nongeni says, catching me off guard. "Why not?" she urges. "Phone them and find out if he is out of prison."

"They are not living behind Mrs. Mcebi's house any longer. I don't know how to find them. They have no phone."

"Phone Mrs. Mcebi. Ask her to contact your parents and tell them you will call again. I'm sure she must know where they are."

I open the window and the sound of our cast singing and dancing in the street below floats into my room. Across the way, people continue cleaning their homes, watering plants, pumping iron.

I close the curtains. I have to know.

It takes three days, probably a hundred dollars, and a lot of patience to set up the phone call to my parents. First there is no one home at Mrs. Mcebi's. Then I get through to the youngest daughter, who can't understand me. Finally I try again and speak to Mrs. Mcebi. She doesn't know where my mother and father have moved to, but she promises me she will find out.

The following day I phone her again. She knows nothing more, because of the huge parties, happiness, and confusion in Soweto. Ask Auntie Somoza, I tell her.

The more I try, the more I want to talk to my family.

On the third day, she tells me that she has delivered the message and that my parents will be at her home tomorrow night, six o'clock, South African time. That means tomorrow morning I will hear my mother and father's voices. I put on my makeup and feel sick at the smell.

The dressing room is silent; everyone is sullen. After the excitement of Nelson Mandela's release, nothing has changed for us. We know there's a big party at home, and we are not part of it. The news here has returned to the American deficit, but all our talk is only of South Africa, Soweto, and home.

Gloria's smoking, with her feet up on the table. Ash falls on her costume. Even she is not interested in the show anymore. All her energy is reserved for her American boyfriend. Tisha's reading an electronics magazine and eating a hamburger. Sipho has brought a portable television into our dressing room and is watching MTV. His father's death is still with him, and it makes him quieter. I have tried talking to him, but he stares at me, shrugs, and switches on the television. No one calls him Sipho-Smiler anymore.

"Come on, everyone, get a move on!" says Josh, coming in.

"Is it time already?"

"Yes, and we're back to full houses again. With Mandela free, everyone wants a part of the new South Africa." He looks at us all. "Come now, my little songbirds. Let's just take it one show at a time, starting with tonight's . . ."

"Another show down," says Gloria.

And only a million more to go!

I stand alone by the phone in my apartment. I have all the numbers written big and clear in front of me. I hit the buttons one at a time, slowly. I don't want to make a mistake. As the last beep sounds there is a pause and then I hear the ringing. I wonder if Phakane will pick up the phone.

"Seraki?"

"Hello, it's me!" I imagine the miles of ocean and land between me and my father standing in Mrs. Mcebi's house. "How are you? Is Phakane out of prison? Is Mom there with you? What is happening?" The questions tumble out.

"Wait, not so fast." He laughs. "Let me answer," and he is talking like I am in the same room with him, like I've just come home from school. "Everybody is fine. Your mother is here. Our new house has a vegetable garden. I'm growing vegetables. I wish you were here to help. Talk to your mother . . ."

"Wait, wait, tell me . . ." But my mother's voice comes on the line.

"Seraki?"

"Ma, how are you?"

"Seraki?"

"Yes, Ma, it's me."

"How are you, my son?"

"I'm fine. Everything is going well. I'm missing you. Listen, Ma, I phoned to find out about Phakane. Here they say that the government is releasing other detainees. What's—"

"Phakane is still in prison," she says, and I feel something deep inside my body let go and fall to my feet. "But the lawyer thinks he will be coming out soon."

"What lawyer?"

"I have a surprise for you, Seraki . . ."

167

I can hear the smile in her voice.

"What?"

"Hey, *mshana!* Howzit in America? You're a big star there yet?"

Uncle? What is he doing there?

"I'm fine, fine. What are you . . . ? What does Father say about . . . ?"

"We are family, Seraki. We sort these things out. Mr. Nzule and I are talking again, aren't we, brother?"

I can imagine Uncle glancing at my father when he says those words to me, and I can see my father looking away, and my mother beaming. I laugh. It's so good to hear these people.

"Tell me about the lawyer."

"It's the money you sent me, Seraki. I couldn't buy the band equipment without trying first to see if I could get my other *mshana* out of prison. Your father and I together got this lawyer who is helping us. He's first-rate. He thinks Phakane will be out soon. With Mandela's release—hey, what a party we are having!—things are looking good. Every opportunity we get we all visit Phakane and tell him the news of you. He is looking well, and has a letter on its way to you."

We talk to one another for half an hour. My father tells me about his job at the Community Center. He has planted a garden there too. Uncle is still without work, but he is playing better music. He wants to play me his latest song over the phone. My mother won't let him. I even talk to Mrs. Mcebi. I don't want to lose these people, but too soon I have to.

"Good-bye, I will write again very soon, I promise."

I look about this empty room. Seconds ago it was crowded with my family. We were together, eating a huge sweet meal. Now my plate is gone, snatched away by the clink of a telephone receiver. I have to leave. Go out for a walk.

"Seraki? Wait for me!" Nongeni calls as I get into the elevator. "How was your phone call? Is Phakane free?"

"I spoke to everyone, even my uncle. Not Phakane, though. He is still in prison. Things are happening, but they still don't know when he will be let out. Uncle says Soweto has been partying night and day since Mandela's release."

"Where are you going now?" she asks.

"Out." I stop the elevator at her floor and hold open the door.

"What about Mosake's rules?"

"His rules make no difference to me."

"Can I come with you? There is something I have to tell you."

"You're not afraid of Mosake?"

"This is more important. Come with me to a coffee shop. I don't want anyone else to hear."

We find a booth at the back of the coffee shop and she blurts out her problem before I can even reach for the menu.

"Yesterday I went shopping with Linda, but I didn't have enough money to buy lunch. She asked me what I was doing with all my essentee."

"Essentee? What's essentee?"

"That's what I asked her. It's S. and T." She draws the letters in the water from under her drinking glass. "It's money that's meant for Subsistence and Travel. An allowance, extra money paid to performers from overseas."

"What? We've never—"

"I know, but she said she saw a receipt last month for it in Bob Haskins' office. It was for the Liberty Globe Theater's S. and T. payment to the *iSezela* cast. It was signed by Mosake!"

"Let's go," I say.

Neither of us talks as we walk back to the Block. We are both too busy thinking the same things. "Hey! Look! The Plant Lady is chucking out her ferns!"

We stop by the alley and look up. She is at her window, pulling her plants from their pots, and throwing them to the pavement. She is crying. A cat dashes away to escape the shower of dirt and brown leaves.

"What do you think we should do now, Seraki?"

"Talk to Arturo's cousin."

"Arturo's cousin?" she asks.

"Yes, Pablo, the lawyer!"

RIPPED-OFF

"Look, I can't say definitely that Mosake's cheating you, because I've no proof. But it certainly looks like there's something odd going on," Linda says, putting her coffee down.

We're sitting in a busy coffee shop, and Nongeni is leaning over the table carefully checking the figures on the papers Linda has brought with her.

Ever since I've known Linda, she has always been tough. Today she looks worried. She must be scared about losing her job. From what she's told us, and from what these papers say, at the very least, this could be embarrassing for the Liberty Globe Theater.

Linda is right. As the host theater, they have paid the subsistence fees they are supposed to. And if we are right, Mosake has pocketed our allowances. By now, that would be a lot of money. Our money.

"The problem here," she continues, "is that Mosake's been very clever. He'll say that he pays for your accommodations, which he does, and gives you pocket money every week."

"Fifty dollars!"

"Nevertheless, he gives you something, and he pays for your dinners after the show."

"That's terrible food," Nongeni protests. "We never eat it."

"It doesn't matter. He'll say he's doing exactly what he agreed to, even though he's probably cut a deal with the owners of the apartment block to save himself some money. You shouldn't be living more than two together." She pauses. "If nothing else, he'll claim that you're underage and that he can't hand over large sums of money to minors."

Nongeni and I look at each other. Linda goes on.

"You did say your parents signed over all authority to him?"

"Half of them probably can't read," Nongeni mumbles.

"I signed my own," I say.

"It doesn't matter. Mosake is your legal guardian in America. He'll claim that he's looking after your best interests."

"He's too busy looking after his own interests to worry about ours!" snaps Nongeni.

"I'm afraid he's covered his tracks very well."

"But what about our salaries? We're not being paid nearly our share for a hit show on Broadway."

"You signed your contracts back in South Africa. You agreed to these terms. The Liberty Globe Theater can't be held responsible for the terms of contracts between artists and private management. I'm sorry, kids, but he's been very clever."

"But he's cheating us!" I say.

"Yes, but he's cheating you legally, Seraki. In New York, that's how the game is played. Everyone's looking for a way to cheat legally, to find the loophole that'll make them rich, while staying within the boundaries of the law. Sometimes these boundaries are stretched to their limits. I tell you what, now that I've spoken to you both, I'll ask Bob about this and see what he says."

"No!" we both shout.

"Don't do that," Nongeni pleads.

"We want to handle this ourselves," I explain. "It's got nothing to do with Bob Haskins, or the Liberty Globe Theater. This is between Mosake and us."

"Seraki's right," Nongeni agrees. "We have to fix Mosake on our own."

"What are you going to do?" Linda asks.

Nongeni and I stare at each other. I don't think she has a plan. I know I don't. Not yet.

"To begin with," Nongeni says, "I guess we should tell the others."

"That's what Pablo said. I saw him yesterday."

"Who's Pablo?" Linda asks.

"One of Arturo's cousins. He's a sports lawyer. He said he doesn't know much about theater law, but that he'd find out all he could."

Linda still looks worried.

"You kids are taking on quite a monster, you know?" She leans across the table and squeezes Nongeni's hand. "But I'll do what I can to help you."

A waitress plonks the bill down, and Linda pays, saying, "Keep the change."

"Have a nice day!" The woman smiles.

"We'll try," says Nongeni, and Linda smiles for the first time all morning.

Nongeni and I track down as many of the kids in the Block as we can find, and tell them what we've learned. They look as if they are listening, but it's as if most of them don't want to hear what we're saying.

Gloria doesn't believe a word of it.

"You don't know what you're talking about, Seraki," she says. "Do you know how much it costs to run a Broadway theater?"

"No, I don't," I admit.

"Well, then! You have no right—"

"But it can't possibly cost seven hundred and twenty thousand dollars a week!"

Most of the kids mumble and protest. I didn't realize how strong Mosake's hold is on them. They can't believe he is cheating them. They are as tired and unhappy as I am, but they are still loyal to him!

"You're just making trouble, Seraki." It's Gloria again. "All you want to do is get back at Mosake. You two are always clashing. Don't involve us in your revenge!" she shouts and slams the apartment door on her way out.

This time I have no comeback. She may be right. Maybe I *am* looking for revenge.

No, I'm not! Nongeni and I know that Mosake is cheating us. What he's doing is wrong. I'm doing this for all of us, even Gloria.

Only Sipho says something different.

"What took you guys so long?" he asks. "I could have told you months ago that he's gone white on us."

Later, in our dressing rooms at the theater, everyone is mumbling and whispering. I look over at Nongeni. At least we've got them thinking.

"Fifty bucks gets you nowhere in New York," one of the boys says to two others.

"Yeah, man. In Soweto it would be a lot of money, but it's nothing here."

"Nobody told us what it was like in New York!"

"And Mosake's used our ignorance to take advantage of us," Nongeni says.

"But we all signed those contracts!" Sipho says. "There's nothing we can do. He owns us."

"But listen a minute. Maybe there is something we can do," I say. "There's nothing in our contracts about the show being extended for six months. Sure, we signed without knowing all the facts, but now we know how big a success this show is."

"And now we know that there's such a thing as a subsistence allowance!" Tisha adds.

"Mosake can't expect that we'll all sign up again." It's Teddy. "Can he?" he asks.

"Maybe not so fast this time," Sipho says.

"Remember Oswald, our financial backer, with his bright orange shirt?" I say. "Remember how quickly Mosake ditched him once the show was a success?"

"That guy was a pig," one of the girls says.

"Right. None of us liked Fat Oswald, but I bet you a rotten week's salary that Mosake dumped Oswald at the first sign that the show was going to be a hit without paying him what he had coming either. Remember that night Mosake and Oswald had their fight backstage?''

''Mosake probably knew then that the show was coming to New York and didn't want to have to share the big bucks,'' Sipho says.

I look at Sipho. He's smiling. He is coming alive again.

''But that's just it,'' says Gloria. ''It's Mosake's show. He created it, he brought us here. He made it happen for all of us.''

Everyone stares at her.

I hope she doesn't go running to tell him. If we can't convince her . . .

''But could he have done it without us?'' I ask her. ''Admit it, Gloria. You couldn't carry the show alone. Without us, there would be no *iSezela!*'' I say it loud. I want those who are in the dressing room to hear me.

The room goes quiet.

''Seraki's right. Without us there would be no Broadway hit,'' one of the boys shouts from the back. ''We're a team . . .''

''Even Mosake said that we all have to work together!'' another boy adds.

Big Joe pokes his head in the doorway. ''Five minutes,'' he says, and his voice sounds real loud in the sudden hush.

''Think it over!'' I say.

As we move toward the wings, I grab Nongeni to hold her back. ''I think they're beginning to realize how stupidly trusting they've been.''

''Can you believe how dumb some of those girls are? They're so cozy in their routines they don't seem to mind that they're being ripped off!'' she says. ''I couldn't believe their reactions. The main thing they're worried about is causing trouble! 'What if Mosake gets angry?' they asked me.''

''What did you say?''

'' 'So what!' I was feeling pretty angry myself.''

''Hey, you two, Seraki and Nongeni, keep it down!'' Big Joe whispers from his corner by the controls. ''We've got clearance from front of house.''

174

"The boys weren't any different, Nongeni, but at least the ones who said it was total rubbish earlier were silent now," I whisper back to her.

"It doesn't matter. Even if, once they finally get some brain cells ticking, all they do is work out how much they could add to their wardrobes . . ."

". . . or how many more televisions they could buy."

"Go, house lights," Big Joe whispers into his microphone.

The audience settles down.

We start another show.

Our performance is terrible, but I mean really terrible! No one seems to have any energy. Everyone is thinking about something else. Even Gloria misses a cue. For the first time the audience doesn't seem to enjoy the show. They hardly applaud at all.

We take off our makeup, drop our costumes over the chairs, and get ready to leave. Tonight no one even looks at the burgers on the table. How was I to know what Nongeni and I said would have such an effect?

We are almost out of the theater when Mosake comes charging backstage.

"What the hell happened to you kids tonight?" he shouts. "Gloria, how could you of all people . . . Sipho, your timing is shocking! All of you, the dancing was sloppy and the singing flat. What is going on with you?"

Nobody answers him. We stare dumbly at one another and continue our packing up. Gloria is the first to walk past him without saying anything. Not even good night. Nongeni and Tisha link arms and follow her. Teddy and Sipho do the same.

I wait. I have to see what happens. I notice that none of the boys looks at him, but that some of the girls do, in a new and different way, like they're thinking, Can he really be cheating us?

Now I am the only one left backstage.

"Seraki, you tell me. What's going on? I've never seen them perform so badly." His tone is confidential, engaging. He wants me to think that I am special to him.

I see through it all. I will give nothing away.

"We're tired," is all I say, strolling down the corridor. I don't look back, but I can feel his eyes drilling through my back.

The following day everyone is buzzing. Teddy stays away from his TV long enough to read the theater pages in the *New York Times*. We are the only show on Broadway playing nine shows a week.

Gloria confides that the other reason Cathy left was because of a money problem with Mosake. Gloria felt bad about telling us. She promised Cathy she would never tell anyone.

Tisha says that Big Joe and his crew have said all along we were crazy to be working so hard.

Tonight's performance is worse than last night's. We are lazy, the pace drags. The audience is not pleased. They see through us, and people walk out before the interval. The tight and lively quality of our show is gone. Getting to the first-act curtain takes forever.

During interval Josh comes backstage.

"What is going on out there?" he asks. "You're worse than zombies. I've never seen you so uninvolved. Somebody talk to me, please!"

"Leave us alone," Tisha says. "It's interval. We've a second half to do and we're getting on with it. Okay?"

Josh stares openmouthed at us. None of us pays him any attention. No one cares about *iSezela* anymore.

"Five minutes to the second act. Crew stand by," Big Joe announces. "Crew stand by."

Afterward, when the polite applause of a half-empty house dies, Mosake is standing at the stage door. This time he doesn't shout. He merely glares at each of us in turn.

We are silent too. We have nothing to say to one another, and not even a look for Mosake.

Josh catches me in the alley outside the stage door. He has nothing to say either, but he hands me a note. From Pablo. He wants to see me "ASAP."

Nongeni says that means "right away."

176

BEWARE OF THE TAIL

Pablo is late. I can't wait for him any longer. I must join the others in the greenroom. We are all here early, but no one is paying any attention to Josh's directions. Nobody seems to care about warming up.

"I'm tired of doing these dumb exercises. They don't make sense anymore!" Sipho yells at Josh.

I look over at Nongeni. She's sitting on the floor and questioning me with her eyebrows. I shake my head no. Pablo hasn't come yet. But he and Arturo should be arriving any minute.

The others are leaning against the mirrors, milling around and mumbling. It looks like Josh's warm-up is never going to happen.

"Kids, please!" he pleads. "You know the routine. Come on, let's get going here. What's wrong with you today? We all know how terrible last night was. We've got to work together to get some of the old magic back."

"Why?" asks one of the boys.

Josh is stunned. He sputters about professionalism, about commitment to the Liberty Globe Theater, about our paying public.

"Why?" repeats Tisha.

"Because this is not just a musical, it's a message." Mosake's voice fills the room. He is carrying his *sjambok*.

We look at him blankly. Now, nobody says anything. No one moves.

"Get up!" he says quietly to Nongeni and the girls around her.

I watch Nongeni. She is watching Mosake. She doesn't stand up, only turns to face the mirror. I admire her courage.

Some of the others wander away from the middle of the floor. No one looks at Mosake. Everyone watches him in the mirrors.

Tisha walks to Nongeni. She whispers something I cannot hear.

"There's no problem, Mosake," Josh babbles, moving quickly from the piano. I feel bad for Josh. He tries. He wants us to be good, and he wants to protect us from Mosake. "Everything's under control," he says. "The kids are just a bit tired tonight . . ."

Mosake stands rigid, flicking the *sjambok* on the greenroom floor. Its long, thick thong, the crocodile's tail, makes soft slapping sounds.

I recognize it as the one he used that night. Sipho moves to the back of the group. He's made the same connection.

"Tell me," Mosake demands, looking directly at Nongeni, "what's going on here?"

She looks back at him without answering.

He turns to me. "Seraki? Answer me! You will answer me now," and the end of the whip grazes my foot.

"So you have forgotten the message of *iSezela?*" Mosake says, walking slowly about the room with the *sjambok* in his right hand, its thong trailing behind him.

"We're warming up for our show tonight," I say "But it's only a show we're putting on, not a message. That died a long time ago." My voice is steady. The others look at me. They must support me.

"Then warm up, properly, as I have taught you!" he orders.

We wait, very still.

"Stand up!" he suddenly shouts, swinging around toward Nongeni. He raises the *sjambok*.

"Mosake, you must stop this!" Josh shouts, but Mosake pays no attention to him. Josh races from the room. We are alone with Mosake, behind a closed door.

Nongeni slowly gets to her feet.

"When I say warm up, you will warm up!" He rushes at us, lashing the *sjambok*. We scatter, but one of the boys is caught on the leg. He falls and the second snap of the thong cracks a mirror. Another boy is caught across the back. He cries out.

178

Mosake turns to face the girls.

"You will do as I say! NOW! Nobody crosses me! Warm up! I said WARM UP!"

"Mosake!" I yell, rushing at him.

He whirls to face me, the thong hissing out at my head. I duck and with all my strength I punch my fist into his stomach.

Strike at the underbelly! Keep away from the tail!

Mosake brings his elbow down hard, catching me on the side of my face. He stands over me, panting.

Gloria is sobbing.

"You! Seraki!" Mosake growls at me. "You have done this!" He raises the *sjambok* again. I roll to escape the lash, but brace myself for the next blow I know is coming. From the corner of my eye, I see Sipho dive. Shoulder first, he hits Mosake in the back. Strike at the underbelly I want to yell to him.

Mosake stumbles and falls forward onto his knees, but jabs backward with the butt of the *sjambok,* catching Sipho hard in the throat.

Sipho is gasping on the floor beside me. Mosake staggers up. Teddy lunges for his knees, and someone else grabs for the *sjambok*.

I scramble to my feet.

The crocodile flails its tail. It grunts, hisses, bites at the boys struggling to hold it. The crocodile is strong. It throws them aside. It strikes again.

I tuck my chin into my chest and join the attack, launching myself head on at his belly.

Strike at the underbelly!

I hear a gasp. I hit the ground. I will strike again.

The *sjambok* is lying near me on the floor. Mosake is doubled over, his face contorted as he scrambles toward me to retrieve it.

The door of the greenroom crashes open, with Bob Haskins pounding through it. Josh and Linda are close behind him.

"What the hell's going on in here?" he roars.

Mosake looks up at him.

"You stay out of this!" he hollers. "These kids are getting what's been coming to them for a long time!"

"Mosake, what are you doing?" Linda cries.

"These kids, they're not working!" He is up on his knees now. Josh is standing over him, shaking silently. He does not reach down to help him.

The girls crowd behind Linda, all except Nongeni. She's still on the floor, crouching by the door. I see her slip past them and disappear down the corridor.

Teddy's nose is bleeding. There's blood on the floor. I see the blood of my father on a different floor. My face is burning.

Bob Haskins strides over to Mosake, snatches the *sjambok* from his hand, and throws it out of his reach.

"Have you gone crazy? You have no right to do this to these kids. How dare you! This could get us into a lot of trouble!" he says fiercely. He looks like he might kick Mosake. I wish he would, but he doesn't.

"You keep out of this," Mosake answers, finally on his feet. "You don't understand. This is what these kids need. They're from Africa, remember? This is what they know and this is what they deserve," he pants. "It's all their fault, the two of them," and he points at me and looks about for Nongeni. "Where is she? I know Nongeni's in this with you, Seraki."

No one answers him, but one by one the kids close in around me. Finally they are backing me up.

"Ask him about the money!" Sipho gasps, with hardly any voice at all, to Haskins. "Ask him about the money. The subsistence allowance he hasn't been paying us!"

He stares at us. We nod, shake our heads yes.

Bob Haskins turns to Mosake, who is wiping sweat from his face with a silk handkerchief. His eyes are still glaring, but only at me. And then he smiles at Bob Haskins, and says, "You have to understand, Bob . . . These kids . . ."

"Yes. Tell me, Mosake. What are they talking about? Tell me about the money."

Nobody in the room is taken in by Mosake's smile.

"I don't know what he's talking about!" he blusters. "I do

everything for these kids! I pay for their accommodations, for most of their food . . ."

"But that's not how it should be!" A new voice breaks in.

I turn around. Nongeni is standing just inside the door, and with her is Pablo.

He comes forward, right up close to Bob Haskins, before he goes on.

"According to the actors' union, all subsistence paid by managements must be given directly to the artists. Hotel accommodations for overseas companies are to be paid by the host theater. You do know that, Mr. Haskins, don't you?" And then he adds, "Forgive me. You are the director of this theater, aren't you? You are the man in charge?"

Bob Haskins flushes, and turns on Mosake. "What the hell have you been up to? Aren't these kids getting their S. and T.?"

"No, they're certainly not," Linda says, and she looks tough again and I like it.

Pablo reaches for Bob Haskins' hand.

"Pleased to meet you. I'm Pablo Queventes. My card."

Haskins looks like he doesn't know what to say for the first time in his life. I like that too.

Pablo goes on, real calm and smooth, his finger pointing at Mosake.

"This guy's not giving them their S. and T., and he's also not paying them even the minimum union wage for Broadway performers. These kids are getting only a hundred and fifty dollars a week. The suggested wage set, may I remind you, by the actors' union is seven hundred and fifty dollars a week."

Strike at the underbelly, my grandfather said.

"This creep's ripping these kids off something terrible. He's what we call a two-timing, stinking, rotten crook!" It's Arturo, smiling from the doorway.

Mosake tries to speak, but no words come. He looks at Linda, but she turns away. He looks at us, and we stare him down. There's no refuge for him. He leaves the room.

181

No one speaks for a long, slow moment.

Then Bob Haskins, jolly and bright, says, "Well, I'm glad that's all sorted out! Mr. Quéventes, I thank you very much for pointing out these irregularities. I assure you I'll do something about them immediately." And then he is the old Bob Haskins again. "But kids, now listen to me. We don't want this leaking out. We're family. I'll look after you. You'll all be compensated. Think for a minute about the size of that check you'll be getting for back pay. It's gonna be a whopper, I tell you. I won't let my kiddos down. Trust me."

Big Joe is in the doorway now.

"Five minutes to curtain," he says, as if tonight is no different from any other night.

"Well, hell," Bob Haskins says, rubbing his hands together and bustling toward the door, "will you look at the time! We've got a show to put on. You'd better shake and rattle, kids. You know what they say—the show's gotta go on!" He laughs.

"Why?" asks Nongeni.

"Why?" He pauses. "Well, Nongeni, because we've only got about twelve hundred people out there waiting to see you, that's all! So let's get a move on . . ."

Again he tries to leave.

"I'm sorry, Mr. Haskins. I'm not performing tonight, or any other night, until I know what my new salary is," Nongeni announces to us all.

"And I'm not either," I say, crossing the room to stand beside her, "until we work out something about our performance schedule. No one else on Broadway is doing nine shows a week. Why should we?"

"But you can't do this!" he sputters. "What about your audience? They're out there, waiting. They love you kids. You can't disappoint them!"

No one answers. I like watching him shake, worse now than even Mosake.

"Who do you think I am, anyway?" he asks Nongeni. "I can't

make a decision like that on my own. It's a matter for the full board of directors. Listen! I'll tell you what . . ."

He turns from her and looks around anxiously for someone else. "I know this has been traumatic for you," he says to Teddy, "but for tonight I'll double your wages!" Teddy shakes his head. "No? Then I'll triple them! How's that? Triple wages for tonight?" He says to Sipho, "You'd like that, wouldn't you, son?" Poor dumb Bob Haskins. He's picked the wrong boy. He'll make no points with Sipho, and calling him "son" was the worst thing he could have said!

But Sipho doesn't lose his cool.

"I'm not performing at all, ever again, Mr. Bob Haskins," he says, "not until I know when I'm going home.'

"Me, neither!"

"Me, too."

"And me!"

Nongeni steps forward.

"None of us will perform again until we're told what we're getting paid, how many shows we're performing a week, and what's happening about the extended season," she says.

"And don't forget, we want to go home," I say.

"It would appear, Mr. Haskins," says Pablo, "that you have a full-fledged strike on your hands. And under the circumstances I think it's justified."

"But what about tonight? Linda, talk to them?" he pleads.

"Sorry, Bob. I may be putting my job on the line, but I think they're right. I'm with them," she says, and comes over to us and tries to put her arms around all of us at once.

Suddenly the mood in the room is triumphant. We are jumping and singing and dancing. We have beaten the crocodile that Mosake used to control us. The *sjambok* lies limp on the floor. We stomp on it. We kick it. No one bends to pick it up. It is a dead myth. It can no longer inspire or terrify us.

We have taken our own first step toward freedom.

A GOOD SEAT AT THE PLAY-OFF GAME

I finish doing what I have to do. I am the last to leave the theater.

For the first time the marquee is dark outside. It's strange to walk past the entrance like an ordinary person while our audience is collecting their refunds at the box office. Listening to them grumble and seeing the unlit theater is bothering me, after the pleasure of our victory. I feel good about what we have done, and at the same time, not so good.

I look at the late edition newspapers on the stand by the subway entrance. I wonder if our cancellation will make tomorrow's papers. I can see the headline in my mind: "Cast Cripples Croc."

I hope nobody tells the press. Bob Haskins for sure won't, and neither will Josh or Linda. Big Joe and his boys will just be glad of the night off with pay, and Mosake probably won't even tell his Diamond Lady. The rest are too happy to even think of it. They've all gone off all over the city to celebrate. Tonight nobody will think about Mosake's rules.

I don't feel like partying. I missed the big party in Soweto. What is our victory compared to theirs? I want to go back to the Block and be alone. We aren't finished with this thing yet. What did Linda say? We are taking on a monster.

Dear Phakane

I don't know how to begin to tell you what is happening here.

What should I tell him? How can I make him understand? He was the leader of something much bigger than this and I wonder . . .

Look where he landed for his efforts. What if the kids get scared off? What if Mosake fires us all? I don't think most of them would have enough money saved up to even buy their tickets home.

I walk to the window and peer at the block across the way. The Plant Lady's window ledge is bare. I can see her wandering about her room. She doesn't seem to know what to do with herself anymore than I do. Maybe I should phone Pablo? No, he said he would be real busy tonight to get ready for tomorrow's meeting. I wonder what that will be like.

I didn't want to be a leader, and now I am and I don't know what to do.

> I wish you were here with me, Phakane, and I wish I had
> Uncle to tell me what to do.

I read what I have written. I don't know what to write and I don't know what to do. I crumple the page and turn on Teddy's TV.

It's nine o'clock in the morning and I am sitting in a meeting between the management of the Liberty Globe Theater and the entire cast of *iSezela*. My hands are wet in my lap.

At one end of this enormous boardroom table are Bob Haskins, three men in business suits I've never seen before, Josh, and Mosake. Nongeni and I have seats at the other end, with Pablo Queventes between us. He looks real sharp today, with an expensive suit and briefcase. The rest of the kids are along the sides. They look real nervous. Only Gloria looks like she's dressed for the opening night of a Broadway show.

I feel real small in this big room, but now I feel better about what we're here for. Pablo told me all about how these meetings work, and I told him all about our problems and the changes we want. This morning we are organized. We're going to fight by their rules, he said, and we are going to win.

I can't help thinking about Phakane, though, and Nelson Mandela, and how long they have been fighting. I know I have to pay attention to all this stuff they are saying, and I don't understand half the big words they are saying it with.

"So, gentlemen, I think we agree that certain adjustments need to be made to the contract originally signed by the cast of *iSezela*," Pablo says.

"Mr. Queventes, the contract signed between Mr. Mosake and the children has no relevance to the management of the Liberty Globe Theater," answers the man in the red tie far away from me.

"Union rules clearly state that—"

"Are they classified professionals?"

"In South Africa, no, but in America, yes."

This isn't going to be easy, and I watch, as one minute Pablo throws the ball to their end of the court. They defend and the game seems to go back and forth, dribbling up and down the table, with each end taking good shots and then stealing the ball from the other. These men in business suits know the rules, they know how to play, and they are fighting hard, giving Pablo a tough time. I can't quite figure out who's making most of the points.

They've been at it for an hour now, and I think we've lost. Time out while each side talks to their coaches. Mosake looks mad down there, and Nongeni and I are just pretending we know what to say to Pablo. On his pad he's written, "No winner yet. Look confident."

And then they are at it again and Pablo is fighting on. He's used to dealing with tough businessmen in the sports world, and from one point to the next it seems to me that he's handling our case like a pro. How long can this go on?

Now Mosake's looking gloomy at his end of the table. He's not calling time-outs anymore, but only shaking his head and writing stuff down on the pad in front of him.

Josh hasn't said a word all morning. He looks like he's ready to go home, and so do most of the kids. Sipho is staring out the window, watching the traffic I can only hear if I listen carefully. I can see on his new watch that we're now coming up to three hours of this. It doesn't feel like a game anymore.

The businessmen look exhausted, and slowly they are packing

their cases and getting up from the table. I look at Pablo. He is standing over me now, waiting for my high five. We are triumphant.

Our salaries are to be increased. We'll be paid all the outstanding subsistence allowances. We'll have Mondays off and only eight shows a week. There will be a seven-week break before the extended season begins. We'll receive a percentage of the profits from the *iSezela* recording. Back in South Africa, a replacement cast will be auditioned and rehearsed to supplement the cast in New York. And best of all:

Dear Phakane

I am coming home . . .

ANOTHER COUNTDOWN

"Nongeni, Seraki, hang loose a minute, will you, please?" Bob Haskins says, as we're about to leave the theater. The show is the old *iSezela* again. Everyone is performing with new spirit since we won our fight, and even Bob Haskins is talking a bit differently to us now. He's never said "please" before.

What now? Nongeni and I glance at each other.

"Ummm, you kids, you're savvy enough to keep this under your hats, aren't you?"

"What do you mean, Mr. Haskins?" Nongeni asks. She's getting to be more like Linda every day.

"I mean, you kids, you're coming back, right? We're all on the same team now, right?"

"What are you talking about?" I ask even though I think I know. I want to see if I can make him sweat.

"Lookee here. Linda said you're a real sensible young . . . woman, Nongeni." He hesitates. ". . . and well you, Seraki, I know I can trust you. You're my main man . . ."

"What's your point?" she asks, not giving him much time for his fancy talk.

"Okay, okay. I see I got to shoot straight with you two. We can't afford this mess leaking out. It's all settled now and you're getting your fair deal. Think how it'd look if anybody was to know you kids were being exploited. I can see it now: 'Big Bad Broadway Enslaves African Youngsters.' Nasty business, I tell you."

"So what do you want from us?" I ask. I've got him squirming now.

"Just a little promise that our little secret will stay that way. No trouble, eh Seraki-old-buddy?"

"Your secret's safe with us," I say real seriouslike and then I wonder what's making Nongeni twitch next to me. "My lips are sealed, unless of course . . ."

"Hey, man. I said 'no trouble,' " and he gives me another one of his punches on my shoulder. "Let's shake on it, man," and we go through the most complicated and messy version of an African Brothers' shake I've ever seen in my life.

"Almost forgot, this came for you, pal." He tosses an envelope at me.

Outside Nongeni bursts out laughing.

" 'My lips are sealed.' Honestly, Seraki, you sound more like an undercover agent in the films than he does."

"Just want him to know that we know how to get back to the underbelly if we need to."

Seraki,

You never told me what you went through to get to see me that time. Thank you, brother—and now it is so easy to have visitors. I see Mom, Dad, and Uncle every week. My situation has changed now that I have a lawyer representing my case. Yesterday I walked out of prison on a day parole and felt sunshine on my back and Soweto dust in my eyes again, and brother does that feel good! The lawyer is hopeful that soon this will become permanent.

I don't know where to start telling you about what has been happening to me in here. But I hope I will see you shortly and we can have a long talk about everything that's happened to both of us.

I am recovering from the hunger strike I was on, but the doctor says I must drink only liquids for a while to get strong again. It was hard not eating for such a long time, but I got a lot of support from other prisoners and even people outside. When I was on the hunger strike, I thought the most about my family. I thought a lot about you. It seemed as though I could see everyone more clearly when I wasn't eating.

Thanks for the money you send back home. It's a great help to Dad and Mom, and me, too, of course. Dad's very proud of you and tells everyone what a successful American you have become! Mom's left her job with her white family and has work as a dressmaker in Soweto. She wants to start her own sewing shop, and they've moved from Mrs. Mcebi's and are now in a proper brick house with running water and lights.

Auntie Somoza came and visited me the other day and told me all about you and King Danny. She told me that King Danny has been caught selling drugs to school kids and will be in prison for the next five years. I thought you would like to hear that.

When are you coming home? Do you want to forget your family? Are you a proper American now? Don't get too American, From your brother, Phakane.

Nongeni and I read the letter over and over again. It's been four months since I was in South Africa, and even longer since that short visit with Phakane last year. His letter has taken a long time getting here.

We pore over the letter and try to imagine all the things that Phakane left out. I cannot let myself hope that he might be at home with me in a few more weeks, but I can't keep myself from remembering things about my brother from before he went to prison.

Like how he taught me to play soccer, and how much I want to teach him to shoot baskets.

When I read his letter out loud it is as if Phakane is standing in front of me talking. It's like a wind has brought the good memories back to me, and Phakane sits warm and snug in the front of my mind.

We have so much to talk about now. I have not been where he has, but now I understand all about crocodiles and we can talk about myths and fears and fighting our fights together. And I hope, knowing I mustn't hope, that we will sit outside in the African sun to do our talking.

Spring's in the air and the days are warmer. Everyone's so happy knowing we are going home! The next two weeks will fly by.

I stand outside the door to our Block. The Lady of the Plants is struggling to get a shopping cart up the steps to her apartment. It is filled with pots of green things, gardening tools, a sack of fertilizer, and an empty window box.

I cross the road to her.

"Aren't they beautiful!" she says, her cigarette bobbing up and down in the corner of her mouth. "Don't ya just love spring and all its pretty little green things! There's not enough of them in this city. Gray, I tell you—that's New York—dull gray! Nothing like a bit of green to cheer you! I just love my plants! I talk to them, you know? It helps them grow."

I can't help bursting out laughing.

She is right—spring is the time to start over again. I hold the door for her.

"You're on the third floor, aren't you?" she says, pointing to my window. "I've seen you! You've gone through quite a rough time lately, haven't you? I know all about you." She cackles while she coughs and lets the door slam behind her.

I laugh too. I never thought somebody could be apartment spotting from the other side!

* * *

After our last show of this season, while the party is still happening in the Block downstairs, Sipho and I push open the trap door and climb the fire escape to the roof.

"Come on, Nongeni," I say. "I promise you, you're going to like this."

"Are you sure we're allowed to do this?" she whispers.

I hold open the security gate that's separating us from the New York night.

"Nobody will know, Nongeni," Sipho says. He has been smiling all day and his grin is taking up almost his whole face.

Slowly they walk around the edge of the rooftop. They are both quiet. Neither of them has ever been up here before or seen this view of the city at night. Below us lies a forest of lights.

Against the dark sky, the huge rectangular buildings have lost their edges. They are only rows and columns of twinkling lights separated on the ground by streams of white headlights and red taillights moving on the busy streets. It all looks like fire flowing between glowing glass candles. Above, the night sky is dotted with stars.

"It's so beautiful," Nongeni says. "From up here you forget what actually happens down there."

"Why have you brought us up here?" Sipho asks.

"Come, this way," and I lead them behind the projecting doorway, the vent pipes, and the trash that's been left up here, to a pile of broken crate wood and cardboard I have heaped in the middle of the rooftop.

"It wouldn't be right to leave without saying a proper good-bye to iSezela," I say, pointing to my perfectly prepared altar. Nongeni and Sipho look at each other and move closer. I light a match.

"What are you doing?"

I don't answer. I want this moment to be as beautiful for them as it has been every time I've rehearsed it in my mind for myself. I sprinkle barbecue fluid over the pile and toss the flickering match. There is a swoosh of blue and orange flame and then a slow and steady crackle as the light and fire build. Behind us our shadows dance on the wall.

"What are you doing?" Sipho asks this time.

"I don't think we will be needing this anymore," and I reach deep into my pocket and hold the crocodile high above the blaze.

"Where did you get it?" Nongeni gasps. "I thought Mosake . . ."

Sipho is staring. His smile is gone. "The last time I saw this was—"

"Yes," I say. "I went back there, Sipho. I found my way through all those tunnels, to the green neon light. And it was still there. It was right where he left it."

"Let me see that thing," Nongeni says, grabbing it from my hand. "I've always wondered how it made you bleed that first day in the rehearsal room."

I laugh.

"That's half of why I went to find it myself. Look, it's nothing but a rusty safety pin stuck through the middle of its stomach. There's no magic to it, Sipho. Take a good look, brother, and when you're ready, the honor is yours."

Nongeni passes Mosake's terrible toy to Sipho, and without hesitating, he throws it onto the glowing embers. It lands dead center, and for an instant it looks up at us just like it used to. Then its jaw begins to sag and its tiny feet flare up as blue flames lick the bronze paint. The eyes pop, melt, and disappear, and the tail curls slowly, pulling it onto its back until it shrivels to nothing. The underbelly is the last to burst into flames, and we watch as our crocodile turns into a gooey black blob.

"Crocodile burning, crocodile burning," Sipho shouts.

We sit around the fire until it burns itself out, and then, as we lean over the parapet, saying our private good-byes to New York, Nongeni whispers,

"Crocodile no more."

FLYING

It's been almost a year since I flew behind that red sports car to the Community Center and boarded the rocket ship *iSezela*. I'm not so keen on the color red anymore, but again I am flying over the dust-brown earth of Africa. It feels like my dream-flying. I am excited, my ears ping, and I can't stop my mind from racing over the familiar faces that I hope will be waiting to see me on the ground.

"We are about to begin our final descent to Jan Smuts International Airport. Ladies and gentlemen, replace your seats and tray tables to their original upright positions and fasten your seat belts, please. We should be on the ground in about twenty minutes. And I'd like to add a special word to the *iSezela* cast. You kids must return to your seats . . . and . . . welcome home. We're proud of you."

There is a loud cheer and so much confusion that I cannot hear the rest of what the captain is saying. It doesn't matter. We are almost home.

"Take my seat, Sipho," Nongeni says, pushing him down the aisle. "I have to talk to Seraki." She collapses into the seat next to me. "I've been trying to talk to you the whole flight. How are you feeling?"

"Like I'm flying."

She laughs.

"I know that, but I mean how are you feeling inside?"

"Scared."

"You! That's the last thing I'd expect to hear from you."

"No, really, Nongeni. What if I've changed so much in the last five months that my family won't know me? Haven't you thought about that?"

"A little," she admits.

"I keep remembering when I was on my way to see Phakane in prison. I was so worried that he would somehow be different. I hadn't seen him in so long and he had been through so much, and . . ."

"Was he different?"

"Yes. And now we've been away a long time, too, and what if . . . ?"

"We have changed, Seraki. You know that. We've done a lot since we left, but remember that South Africa has changed too. Everything has changed—and yet we'll all pick up from where we left off and everything will be fine."

I hope she's right.

"What's Sipho going to do about the show?" she asks.

"He signed a contract in New York, for six more months."

"He did? But we don't have to decide until the end of this month, after the new kids have auditioned!"

"I know. But now that his father's dead he has to support his family. He's not happy about the idea of going on with the show, but he said he can't throw away so much money. He was afraid that once he got home he'd change his mind."

I look at Nongeni. She seems worried.

"He's okay. He's real strong now. Mosake can't do anything to hurt him anymore. And you'll be there to look after him . . ."

"And you? Have you decided?" she asks.

"No. I have to try to get Phakane out of prison first. This time I can't think about going to New York until he is free. Once he's free, then I can return, if I still want to."

"What if Mosake won't renew your contract? He might not, you know?"

"I know, and I honestly won't care if he does leave me out. I'll miss the show, and Arturo and Josh and you, and Sipho, but I certainly don't want to be an actor all my life. I've got more important things to do."

"I've thought about that, too. Josh offered me Cathy's old job as company manager with the new show. Linda said I should take it. She said it could lead to big things for me, but just when I was about to say yes, Gloria announced she was marrying that dude and moving to California."

"Which dude?" I ask. I gave up long ago trying to keep track of them all.

"Her latest one, I forget his name. And then Mosake offered me her part. I wanted to talk to you about it, but you were off playing basketball. So I decided all on my own." She pauses, like she's thinking it through one more time. "No matter what I think of Mosake, I can't refuse the offer. Performing is all I've ever wanted to do."

"I think it's great. Don't feel bad about it. We should all be doing exactly what we want to do."

"And at least if you're not there, I'll still have Tisha. She signed on again—did you know that?—but only because she's also going to start a course in technical theater at the university. Big Joe set it up for her. She doesn't really want to sing, she's been blinded by the lights—literally."

"That's great! She'll be good at it, and having been a performer, she will understand what it's like when she's the big boss of all those controls."

"Look! There's the airport," Sipho shouts from a couple of seats behind us. Peering out the window, I catch a glimpse of the terminal as the plane makes its final turn to the runway. In a few seconds we'll be standing in Africa. We will be home.

The airplane tilts, then levels out, and the ground disappears. With a slight jolt and bump, we touch down and the engines roar, pulling us forward in our seats. There's another long round of cheering until the plane slides to a stop in front of the terminal. A huge poster—"Welcome Home *iSezela* Cast!"—is draped over the balcony, fluttering in the wind.

Once the cabin doors open, we tumble out of the airplane, down the steps and into the warm air of Africa. I feel it on my face, I smell it in my nose, and I want to stand here forever and feel this sun.

A large crowd is gathered on both sides of the banner. They are waving at us. Is that Cathy standing there waving like her arm will fall off? I wonder who I'll see first—Uncle, Mom, Dad?

After a short wait at the passport control, we scramble for our luggage, which revolves around a conveyor belt, pass through the green channel of customs—someone, maybe Cathy?—has done something so we don't have to have our bags pawed through—and head for the airport foyer.

It is a wall of people, faces, everyone excited, looking, craning their necks. Nongeni runs past me into her father's arms. I look for my family. They must be here!

I wrote them that this was the day. What if they didn't get my letter? I turn from side to side, looking everywhere at once. I drop my bags and jump onto the railing, climbing to scan the crush of people. It is too confusing and too loud with excitement that isn't mine.

Then I hear it. A saxophone, coming from the far end of this enormous, bustling room.

"Uncle!" I see him near the front doors, standing next to my mother and my father. I shout, "Uncle! Mom! Dad!" And they turn and see me. They are coming toward me, and I jump down from the railing.

"Uncle!"

"Mshana!"

"Seraki! You are home, my son, you are home," my mother says, crying.

I am grabbed from behind and smothered in a mountain of bosom smelling of beer. Auntie Somoza. Her laugh is booming, blocking out all the other noise.

"Yo! Yo! Yo! Seraki, how you have grown!" she says, slapping my back.

"Auntie! What are you doing here? Did you get my letters?"

"My son! My son!" My father rescues me from Auntie's arms, and swings me around. My heart is bursting.

"You are home, my son. You are home."

"I know, it's hard to believe." I look over his shoulder for the last face that would put my whole family here with me.

"You have all your bags, *mshana?*" Uncle asks. "Come, let's go. Wait till you see the car we have borrowed to take you home. Red, fire-engine red, and with a driver, no less!" He is laughing as he fumbles through the door with his sax and all my bags. He's not doing it smoothly like Arturo would, and then I don't think about that anymore.

Waiting by the curb is a red car, and, standing a little to one side, just like those fancy New York chauffeurs always stand, is someone I almost recognize.

My brother? I look to my family. They are smiling. Auntie Somoza is cackling and jiggling like she's going to shake into pieces right here on the pavement.

Is this true? But how?

"Don't you know me anymore, little brother?" he says, with the old sparkle in his eyes.

"Phakane?"

"And who else did you think it would be?"

"How? When?" But none of my questions matter. My brother has been brought back to me. He is no longer a memory in a room with high walls, with only a square of sky. He is standing in front of me, in front of the wide blue African sky.

I walk slowly toward him, take his hand, squeeze it. We are the same height. His eyes are level with mine. I run my hand up his skinny arm, and onto his shoulder.

He laughs.

"You think I'm a ghost? Feel this flesh of mine. Mom's putting it back fast as she can."

"But how?"

"It happened a week ago. All the charges have been dropped. I have served my time in the old South Africa. Now we move forward to new things. Fifteen others from my block were all freed in one day. So many good things are happening in this country,

Seraki, so many good things!'' Phakane says, throwing an arm around my shoulder.

And we are hugging each other, at first gently and then more fiercely. And we are jumping up and down, until I lift him from the ground and twirl him around me.

''America has made a man of you, little brother!'' He laughs. ''You have become a man of the sky, but I am still a son of the earth! Put me down.''

I punch my fist into the African sky and sing to my family, to my brother, to the new man that I am, and to the new South Africa that is my home.

About the Author

MICHAEL WILLIAMS grew up in South Africa. He has been a teacher in Kathmandu, Nepal, an assistant producer for New Sadler's Wells Opera in London, and a theater professor on board a ship for the University of Pittsburgh's Semester at Sea program. He is currently an opera producer for the Nico Theatre in Cape Town, South Africa. Mr. Williams has been active in bringing opera to schoolchildren in the townships, using his own compositions based on South African folklore. These include *The Milkbird* and *The Seven-Headed Snake*.

Mr. Williams has published two young adult novels in South Africa.